LADY HELENA'S SECRET HUSBAND

Elizabeth Beacon

MILLS & BOON

Prologue

Spring 1809

'We did it, Will, we're married,' Lady Helena Harborough murmured and nestled her head against her new husband's shoulder with a blissful sigh. 'Despite Mama's hysterics and my father and brother threatening to kill you if you ever came near me again, we are wed and I am so happy.'

'Me, too, my darling,' Will said and pulled her even closer, but he went on staring at the hedges heavy with hawthorn blossom, fields full of yellow buttercups and drifts of creamy white cow parsley lining the roadside outside.

He was trying to pretend it was impossible to make love in a hired carriage, but she knew it wasn't. The great gallant idiot wanted to wait until they got to the secluded cottage her best friend Kate, Lady Herridge, had lent them behind her husband's back for a whole lovely week of honeymoon before Will would have to rejoin his regiment.

Without Kate's help it would have been so much harder for them to marry in secret and Helena smiled at the thought of her friend, who was currently pretending to enjoy a few weeks in Harrogate with her best friend Lady Helena while Kate's husband was away in London. Kate would manage to fool everyone into believing that her friend had taken to her bed with a mysterious illness while Helena enjoyed herself in Will's arms because Kate could be superbly arrogant when she chose to be and nobody would question her insistence on nursing her sick friend herself if she told them not to.

It was all a front, of course; she and Kate had been partners in mischief since their first day at school and Helena trusted her completely. Somehow Helena would get back into her imaginary sick bed without anyone knowing she was ever out of it, if she could not persuade Will he needed to take her with him when he went back to war. She frowned and tried not to doubt she could manage that even after their blissful week of loving. Will needed her every bit as much as she needed him but he had far too much self-control for her peace of mind. He had used it to fight this powerful, very mutual need for a whole month after they met. In the end she had lost patience, tugged him into a darkened room at a very dull party and made him forget his silly scruples in her eager arms.

It was all very unladylike and part of her was still shocked that coolly composed Lady Helena Snowe could be so wanton, but he was worth every risk of their tryst with the *ton* so dangerously close by. She would do anything to be by his side for ever and since passion had flared so hot and bright between them that night she had been longing to do it all over again. It was Will who had insisted on waiting until they were wed for more so it was no wonder she was desperate for him now.

Silly man, she thought fondly as the familiar, sensuous ache nagged at the heart of her even more insistently than usual when he was close by. A shock like warm lightning had run through her the first time they met and it felt as if her senses had truly come alive that night and now her inner woman was so *hungry*. Of course Will had to heal fully after the bullet wound he took at the Battle of Corunna, but now he was well again they had so much loving to make up for. She felt as if she needed to store up as much of it as they could fit into a whole delicious week before he risked a French bullet or sabre blow again. No, she *would* not worry about his dangerous profession on their wedding morning. She had promised herself a whole week of loving and being loved without that fear looming over them at every turn and she must not ruin the blissful days and hours ahead with it now.

'I should never have let things become so heated between us that I lost all my self-control,' he told her gruffly.

'You think it was a mistake, don't you?' she said, every nerve she had on the alert for his admission they had only got married because he was her first and only lover.

'Of course not, but you are a wonder I don't deserve.'

'Yes, you do and true love is not deserved,

it simply happens. I found that out the night we met and I thought you did, too.'

'I love you as I never thought I could love anyone, let alone a titled lady, Helena,' he told her with a rueful smile and an intense, wanting look that reassured her this was true and right, and he was just being gallant and Will in not wanting to make love fully to his new wife without complete privacy.

'Titles don't matter and we *are* on our honeymoon so why should we wait, Will? Newlyweds like us have a licence to make love whenever the opportunity arises and I do believe it's arisen right now,' she said with a wicked, gloating smile.

'Oh, yes, I want you all right, my lady,' he said hoarsely, but his muscles were rigid with his steely determination to resist it.

'Your lady, indeed—I am Lady Helena Harborough now,' she told him, 'and there are blinds on the carriage windows.'

She felt the fine tremor of need in his leanly powerful body, but he still frowned and shook his head. 'No, we must wait,' he said tersely.

'Why? It was perfect without a bed last time,' she argued, hoping it had been for him as well. What if it wasn't? What if he only married her because he felt he had to? No, he could never have made her first time so right and fiery and satisfying if he was just sating his pent-up need for a woman and almost anyone would do.

'We could easily have been caught behaving so scandalously that night. It was reckless and stupid to risk doing what we did in a stranger's house with a ball going on nearby, Helena. I should be shot for so nearly ruining you.'

'No, you shouldn't and don't even talk about being shot again after you were at Corunna,' she said and bit back panic at the very thought of him going into battle again. 'And I don't feel ruined. That night I felt refined and newly made and glorious, do you think that makes me an abandoned hussy?'

'No, it makes you delicious and utterly desirable,' he said gruffly and went back to studying the scene outside as if every flower, bird and tree in blossom along their way had to be counted.

She could still feel the fine tremble of desire in his sleekly muscled body and there was a faint burn of colour on his high cheekbones to say Captain William Harborough wanted his new wife very badly indeed. They only had a week to love blissfully and completely so why must he insist on wasting even a precious hour of it like this? Drat, she wasn't meant to think about the shortness of it until their week was up. Better to live in the moment while they still had it and spring was heady and lush all around them. She almost purred at the feel of him at her side, fit and healthy again under his dashing soldier-in-disguise superfine cutaway coat. He truly had remade her world, though, and she could not face the thought of it without him.

'You will take me with you when you rejoin your regiment, won't you, my darling?' she said, so airily he should agree without even thinking about it.

'No,' he said tightly instead. Steely Captain Harborough flattened the sensitive curve of Will's intriguing mouth, but she refused to let him win.

'I promise not to wilt in the Mediterranean sun or be a confounded nuisance to you and everyone else,' she said. 'But I cannot stay home twiddling my thumbs while you fight and this gives me a right to share the good and bad with you from now on,' she said, holding up her left hand so they could both see the broad gold band he had placed on her wedding finger less than an hour ago. It was still such a wonderful novelty she was almost distracted by the heady promises of it, but now she had raised that taboo subject there didn't seem much point in trying to pretend it wasn't always at the back of both their minds.

'There are aspects of life in the field I would not share even with the rogues under my command if I didn't have to.'

'Ah, but they don't love you. I do, so never mind the mud and heat and all the horrors you want to shield me from, I am ready to weather any hardship that comes along as long as I can do it with you.'

'Life on the march is too hard for even the strongest-minded of ladies. We forge on day after day in scorching sun or endless rain or bitter cold and often, when we do stop, there is no food or shelter or a safe place to sleep. You would hate me for exposing you to such hardship after a while and, as I will never do that, arguing about it is futile.'

'You wouldn't be exposing me to anything. I *want* to go.'

'Which proves you have no idea what you would be letting yourself in for, but I do, my love. Because I have seen and felt and endured it, you will not be able to seduce or coax or argue me into doing what you want this time. *My* wife will not and cannot suffer the terrors and privations the women with us suffered during our retreat from Madrid to Corunna this last winter.'

But it was impossible for her to sit at home waiting to hear if he had been wounded again or, heaven forfend, killed. This blissful, unexpected happiness would slip through her fingers like gossamer if she let it and maybe, if they loved often enough, explored each other's thoughts and hopes deeply enough for a whole week, he would realise they were always going to be better together than apart. She shot him a sultry look as sweet longing sang inside her. He was here now and she loved him so much. Kneeling on the seat, she swayed lithely to the roll of the carriage and stared down into his dark eyes with everything she felt for him on show.

'Kiss me, Will; I need you so much,' she told him huskily. 'Pull down the blinds and make love to me before I faint from frustrated desire,' she murmured as heat knotted her core so urgently it was almost painful. She slicked her tongue over her hungry mouth—surely he could see the pebble hardness of her nipples even through the silky velvet of her pelisse and airy muslins. They felt hot and eager for his touch and tongue, and she ran her hands over his torso, battled the tiny buttons on his fine wedding waistcoat and, as her fingers fumbled with clumsy eagerness, heard him rasp in a great breath and knew this time she had won.

'Behave yourself, Wife,' he said all the same, but she could see a blaze of heat and need in his dark, hungry gaze, watched his pupils flare, then contract with need as she slid her hands further down his delightfully male body, all the time keeping her avid gaze bold and inviting on his.

'Stop treating me as if I am an expensive ornament to be kept in a silk-lined box, Will.

I need you right now; I shall never stop needing you if we live to be ninety. You make me feel so much, so totally, delightfully wanted and wanting. I thought I simply could not love like this until I met you and you proved me wrong. So, this is your fault. I need to do the lovely things we did that night at the ball again right now. I believe it's your husbandly duty to repeat them lest I collapse from wanting you inside me so much, proving you love me as only you can; if you will just get on with it and let propriety go hang for once.'

'Not once but twice,' he reminded her huskily, but his gaze had gone hot and hazy and his knuckles were white with the effort of keeping his hands off her so blatantly willing body.

For a panicked moment that fierce restraint gave her a terrible premonition of her being left so desperately alone at the end of their week. Even thinking of it made tears sting her eyes, but she forced them back. He was here, watching her with hotly eager eyes, so fit and alive it was wrong of them not to enjoy every single moment they did have together to the full.

'Well, I love you too much to be careful,' she said and bent even closer so he could not deny her absolute need of him. 'I am two and twenty, Will, not a spoilt little girl eager to play with her new toy. I shall only ever love you, so why won't you just get on with it?'

'I cannot take you with me, Helena,' he said even as his gaze went feverish with longing and she let her tongue explore her hungry lips to test his resolution even more. 'And I don't want to take you nearly in public again *because* I love you. I love you too much to expose you to the horrors of war as well, so please stop trying to argue and seduce me into doing something I never will, my Helena.'

'You have no idea how hard it would be for me to have to sit home waiting for news of you after every battle or skirmish reported in the newssheets,' she protested, but cool reason argued *what if worrying about you on the march or in camp made him careless of his own safety? What if he was killed searching for comforts you would never want at such a price?*

She knew he would do that, even if she begged him not to, the stubborn great idiot, and so she sat again, knowing she might have to face being left behind after all. She didn't want him to see defeat in her eyes instead of love and urgent desire, though, and besides, she wasn't ready to concede defeat just yet.

'I could not endure seeing you starve or have to fear your capture or appalling abuse from the enemy or even our own men—rebellious and foul as some of them were last winter.' He ran a shaking hand over her tawny curls, smoothed down for the wedding, slipping out the spray of flowers Kate had pinned into her elegantly cropped hair before she stood as witness to their secret wedding along with the local verger. 'I love you too much to risk even a hair on your head, let alone all the things you should never have to see or do if you came with me,' he told her. He gently cupped the back of her head so she had to look at him again even with the stupid tears standing in her eyes she refused to let fall.

'You can't love me too much, Will, it's impossible. I love you with everything I am,' she whispered shakily, resting her forehead against his. 'I can fire a pistol and my brother taught me to ward off a man's unwanted attentions so I am not helpless.'

'You didn't escape mine.'

'They weren't unwanted,' she said huskily and his gaze went molten again.

'I want you so much,' he confirmed unsteadily, love and a twist of humour and all that hot desire heady in his wickedly compelling dark eyes. Perhaps one short week could hold her hopes and dreams and sanity together until he was home again—perhaps. He eyed her hard-peaked nipples and lushly parted lips with a wolfish grin and met her gaze again with a blazing hot look of absolute desire in his own.

'Promise you will never love another woman as you love me?' she said, suddenly unsure of a love she had thought so sure and unshakeable when they had made those vast promises to one another before God only this morning.

'I shall never love anyone *but* you.'

'Good, and don't you ever dare die on me, William Harborough. I would pine away without you until I was nothing but a pale grey stick.'

'I refuse to imagine it; you are the only woman for me, now and always.'

'And I love you so much it hurts, Captain.'

'Then we must be doing something wrong,' he said with a wicked grin.

He must have decided loving her was more important than sparing the coachman's blushes after all since he kissed her so passionately they both forgot it was daylight and everything else but making love.

They did that so often during a sunlit week of loving blissfully Helena almost forgot it was so cruelly short until the last morning when she woke up and discovered he had already gone. He had left a passionate, guilty letter of farewell on the pillow telling her he could not bring himself to say goodbye and walk away from her, so he did it while she slept.

Chapter One

August 1815

'How can you even suggest such a thing, Helena? What an *infamous* idea—my only daughter act as an unpaid governess to a pack of unruly children who are not even related to us? I cannot—no, I *will* not agree to you leaving your own family for such a shabby little life as that,' the Dowager Countess of Pensham insisted as if the very notion might drive her into an early grave. 'It was bad enough when your brother insisted on farming the Home Farm himself and you took to riding about the estates without even a groom to lend you countenance, but now we are in funds again you could at least let me enjoy a little peace before I die.'

Her mother was robustly healthy under the fretful moods and imaginary illnesses, but Helena could hardly blame the Dowager for finding comfort in them after her husband died. That was when they had found out he was on the brink of bankruptcy, but at least it allowed Helena to be busy, since they lacked the means to employ anyone much and her brother's vast entailed and encumbered estates needed to be hauled out of River Tick somehow. Now that things were so much better Helena was bored and restless and so horribly lonely.

Her brother's estates were turning a profit at last and her sister-in-law ran his houses better than the Dowager ever bothered to. Edward would make very sure he never had to live on Queer Street again, but he didn't want his sister acting as his land steward and right hand. Now he could afford a steward and secretary, he seemed to expect his sister to go back to being a lady of leisure with a sigh of relief when really she was so bored she could scream.

'Think how much easier your life will be without the worry of finding me a husband,

Mama,' she managed to joke, although the very thought of one almost made her reassuring smile wobble. 'I am on the shelf, Mama, and you know how little patience I have with the social round nowadays. You will do so much better without me to spoil your enjoyment of it,' she added encouragingly.

No point explaining she was already as married as she was ever going to be, not when Will's name had been listed among the dead after the Battle of Bussaco in the year 1810. The stark words *killed in action* still ached like a raw wound that refused to heal, but if she went to Herridge Hall to help Kate with her late husband's estate and tribe of young children at least she would be busy again.

Kate was the one in need of help and comfort this time so at least she could pay back a little of the steadfast support Kate had given her and it would be bliss not to have to pretend. She hated knowing her best friend was enduring the same dreadful blankness living without *her* beloved husband and she could help Kate while trying not to hurt her own family.

'You have Cousin Flora to keep you company and you will dote on your first grand-child when Edward and Mattie's baby is born, Mama. I know how sorry you were when Lady Herridge was widowed with four little children so I am sure in time you will agree that this is an ideal solution.'

'I sympathise with her, of course, but you are the daughter of an earl, a lady in your own right. Maybe you are no longer in the first flush of youth, but you are Lady Helena Snowe and you even have a dowry again now. There is still time for us to get you established in a household of your own before it is too late.'

'I have spent nearly five years being useful and making decisions, so why on earth would I give up all that to be a reluctant husband's chattel, Mama?'

'Chattel? What nonsense! I always said no good would come of you acting as your brother's land steward, but neither of you bother to listen to your poor mother.'

'We could not afford to, Mama.'

'Maybe not then, but all is well again with us now. You owe it to your family to stay and enjoy the joy dear Ned and his heiress have brought us and I cannot imagine why you would want to desert us at such a happy time. Why must you always be so stubborn and *difficult*, Helena?'

'I don't mean to be, but you and Edward can manage without me now and Kate really needs my help. I am not good at being idle and ladylike nowadays and I dare say it will be a relief not to have to worry about what I will do or say next once you have got used to the idea, Mama.'

'Oh, how I wish your poor, dear papa had not been so very *unlucky* at the card tables. Being away from town for so long has made you so set in your ways. If only we still had Snowe House you would have had a proper chance to marry and have your own children long ago and this foolish idea would never have occurred to you.'

'I had plenty of time to find a husband before Snowe House was sold, Mama. I refused all the eligible gentlemen who asked me to marry them back then and would only have disappointed you if we had been able to spend every Season in town.'

'Impossible girl,' her mother said resent-fully.

Helena told herself it wasn't quite a lie be-cause Will had not been eligible when she certainly didn't refuse *him*. He was a serv-ing officer with a reputation for hard drink-ing, riotous living and kicking up outrageous larks when he was not on campaign and about as ineligible as a gentleman could get. How ironic that the three strong men standing be-tween him and the uncle who held the family carldom had died since then and she might even have been forgiven for marrying Will by now if only he was still alive for her to be married to.

As it was, she supposed the earldom would lapse and the estate would be handed to the Crown when Will's uncle died, though she refused to feel guilty about not giving Lord Flamington an heir. She had been bereft enough on her own account not to want to think about the Harborough succession when her courses arrived a few days after Will left.

'Impossible or not, I am definitely on the shelf,' she insisted anyway, 'but Edward and Mattie are looking forward to a very happy event and, as I said, you have Cousin Flora to keep you company. Kate needs me.'

'But that's even worse, Helena. When you rode out day after day here it was shocking enough, but at least you were doing it on our land for your own family.'

'It is as well I never married, then, since my unladylike behaviour was sure to have shocked the poor man rigid,' Helena said with her fingers crossed as she told two lies in one. Will had loved her at her most unladylike and she had once been very married to him indeed.

'Better a sorely tried husband than remain a spinster all your life, my girl.'

'No, and I am not a girl; I refuse to marry simply for the sake of being married and I am as weary of the whole wretched business as you must be at heart.'

'Then simply stay here and keep me company.'

'You have Cousin Flora now; you do not need me as well,' she repeated for a third time.

'You always did think more of Lady Herridge than you do of your own family,' her mother said and now Helena could see she had offended her mother and she had never wanted to hurt her, just to stop hurting quite so much herself.

'I love you, Mama, but you know how hard the last few years have been for all of us. Maybe a few months away from one another will allow us to see the way ahead more clearly.'

'A message for Lady Helena,' their footman announced solemnly from the doorway.

'Thank you, Bartholomew,' she said, relieved his interruption had stopped them arguing in circles.

'His Lordship has sent the carriage, Your Ladyship,' Bartholomew added, so Helena supposed she had better see what her brother thought was so urgent.

'Tell Lustry to put the tongs to heat and find my best Norwich shawl,' her mother ordered, also looking delighted by the interruption.

'I am to go alone, Mama,' Helena said after reading the brief message from her brother and frowning over his lack of a reason for it.

'Ridiculous, whatever do you two need to say to one another that I cannot hear?'

'Some tiresome leftover business concerning the estate, I dare say. Never mind, Mama, Cousin Flora will be home soon and eager to tell you who she has met in the village today and which of our neighbours are up in the world and which are down.'

'At least she brings me news as I am far too frail to stride about the place like you and Matilda and she certainly should not be doing so in her condition. I am so relieved that I offered dear Flora a home when her rascally husband died, although you two argued against it.'

'Yes, it was a very good notion,' Helena replied solemnly, thinking about the fact that it had taken her and Edward and Mattie weeks of trailing the idea, then shaking their heads to say it was probably not a good one, in order for her mother to finally decide it was hers in the first place.

Helena was still smiling at her mother's gift for changing the facts to suit herself as the carriage drew up at the wide steps of the grand, neo-classical mansion her brother called home. It was time to find out what Edward was in such a bother about.

'What an intriguing summons,' she said, strolling into her brother's favourite sitting room still undoing her bonnet ribbons.

'More of a request than a summons, I hope,' her brother said as she tossed her not at all fashionable hat and gloves on to a handy chair and returned his kiss of greeting.

Edward nodded towards the other side of the room to say they had company. The stiff-backed stranger was standing so still it was no wonder she had failed to see him at first glance. Now she felt a superstitious shiver run down her spine like iced water and took a second look. He was so coldly withdrawn she might just as well have not been here for all the notice he had taken of her. Now she wished she had ignored Edward's request to get here as soon as possible and be sure she was alone. Yet, somehow, she could not take her eyes off the aloof stranger at the window long enough to quiz her brother about his presence.

Silence stretched in the quiet room and the stranger still lacked enough manners to turn and face her. He could at least have mumbled a few words of greeting before going back to his study of Edward's fine grounds. Instead, he stood so stiffly aloof over there that she might as well not exist. She should go, but somehow she couldn't make herself do it and she had the oddest feeling in the pit of her stomach because there was something so achingly familiar about this man who was so busily pretending he wasn't here. She shivered again; how absurd of her to feel so chilled on a fine August day.

If the stranger was trying not to intrude on a family greeting, then why *was* he here in the first place?

Had Edward suddenly decided to join her mother's campaign to marry Helena off to anyone who would have her before she was at her last prayers? No, he would never do that to her, not after being paraded in front of every heiress the Dowager could track down like a prize poodle before he met Mattie and fell in love with one anyway.

Helena shot another look at the stranger's back. Luckily for him he had the height, broad shoulders and leanly narrow waist to do justice to the fashion for gentlemen to wear a cutaway coat with tightly fitting pantaloons or riding breeches. Yet while he looked the part of a country gentleman, he did not act it. It was as well he still had his back turned to her now, though, so he could not see her tremble of unwanted awareness of such a supple and manly form.

What on earth was the matter with her? Lady Helena Snowe had not felt even a whisper of sensual curiosity towards any strange men since the day she first laid eyes on her late husband. She was quite immune to broadly masculine shoulders and an air of arrogant self-confidence, yet her gaze lingered on his averted back as if he fascinated her.

There was an air of impatient vigour about him to give a lie to the salting of grey over his sooty, impatiently short locks. Unwanted heat uncurled inside her even as the rest of her felt even colder because there was something so familiar about the set of his head on his broad shoulders that her heart ached and grief threatened even harder than usual. It was only a fleeting impression of whipcord strength held in check by a steely will fooling her into thinking impossible things were possible after all.

'Won't you sit down, Nell?' her brother said anxiously.

At last she realised Edward was watching her with dread and something like shock—as if he couldn't quite believe what this mystery man had told him. The stranger kept his gaze firmly on the artfully devised landscape on the other side of the window glass and how ridiculous of her fingers to flex as if they wanted to explore his masculine warmth in intimate detail. No! How could she even want to explore him like a lover? She had hurried here too quickly, that was it. No wonder she was breathless and on edge and imagining things that simply could not be true.

'I promised Mama I would not be long,' she told her brother. 'It was the only way to stop her coming with me.'

A wary glance at the still figure by the window and her brother said, 'Are you sure you won't sit down, Nell?'

'Quite sure. Mama will order the gig to see what she's missing soon so we must do whatever you think we have to before she gets here.'

'Aye,' the gentleman finally spoke in a gruff

voice that sent even icier shivers through Helena's body until she wondered if she had the ague.

He sounded nothing like the fashionably drawling beau Will once affected to be in public so she had no idea why every nerve in her body was prickling with awareness while her mind screamed, *No, this cannot be*.

Then he turned and she felt the earth shift under her feet. He met her gaze with unreadable dark brown eyes, but at least now she knew hers must be deceiving her. He might share high cheekbones, an arrogant Roman nose and a mouth made for better things than setting in a grim line, but he wasn't her Will. She gazed numbly into his hard eyes and an older and grimmer face than Will's would be if he really had returned from the dead by a latter-day miracle. This man didn't look as if he even believed in miracles, so how could he possibly *be* one?

'Will?' she whispered all the same.

The ghost nodded but, no, this was just a cruel dream. She must have drifted off in her mother's stuffy drawing room and her weary mind had cruelly made up a Will with all the

verve and fire sucked out of him to punish her
for wishing so hard that she could stop missing him. Clearly, it was time she woke up.

'No, you can't be,' she told the spectre.

'Yet here I still am,' it replied flatly.

She moved closer to test her conviction that
her hand would pass through him and gasped
with shock when his came up to meet it and
now he even *felt* real. His hand was warm and
alive—Will's hand, palm to palm with hers!
Yes, there were new calluses and a scar, but it
felt so familiar her head began to spin.

His eyes were so guarded and his fingers
didn't curl around hers as they used to, as if
they had a mind of their own and together was
where they belonged. She frowned at the idea
she was mourning a man who was not even
dead, but her love would never be so cruel
to her. Since Will could not have done such
a thing to her then her eyes and hand and all
her senses must be deceiving her.

'Will?' she whispered again anyway.

'Helena,' he said softly.

Their hands were still palm to palm, as if
they had better memories than they did. This
close up the dusting of silver over his raven

locks seemed strange on such a young man, but it *was* his warm skin under her fingers. Will's dark eyes *were* looking at her out of a stranger's face. Even her brother's tense silence told her this was Will and the impossible could happen.

Chapter Two

Will watched the vital spark waver in his wife's clear grey eyes as she stared back at him as if she had suddenly decided to believe he was alive after all. Her slender hand went limp and cold against his and he felt her sway. 'I have her,' he barked at his reluctant host, fighting the urge to shout, *mine!* As if she had ever been anyone but her own person, he argued with himself as she resisted his hold on her, then seemed to decide being supported by him was better than toppling over.

'I am *not* going to faint,' she murmured groggily. 'I never faint.'

'Of course you don't,' he said, fervently hoping she was right.

'And I am not going to start now,' she told her brother earnestly, as if she would rather talk to him than this spectre on the wrong side of the grave.

Will walked her to the *chaise* and sat down with her in his arms because he wanted to hold his wife again so very badly. He had worked so hard to stand aloof from his own kind and it should be easy for him to keep doing it, but one touch of her hand, or a reproachful, bewildered look from complicated grey eyes, and he wanted her like—well, like her, he supposed hazily; just the way he always had and that was far too much.

'Do you need brandy…a lavender-soaked cloth?' he asked as he tried to gauge her grasp on her senses from the feel of her rigidly held body.

'Of course I don't, you idiot,' she told him as if his almost panicked concern only added to his villainy.

'What, then?' he demanded gruffly.

'Peace,' she said on a long and heartfelt sigh.

'If you mean leave you in peace and go away again, I am afraid that I cannot oblige,' he said, resisting the urge to loosen his neckcloth under her coolly sceptical gaze. 'And when did you get so thin?' he added as if this was a run-of-the-mill reunion between a soldier and his exasperated wife.

'Now, then, do let me think,' she said ominously. 'Would that be when my husband lied that hc was dead, or when I was so busy helping my present and *truthful* brother pull our family fortunes back from the brink?'

'You *are* feeling better.'

'Yes, I am, so kindly let me go,' she demanded and Pensham stared at them with brooding condemnation in his not nearly as pretty Snowe grey eyes.

'No, it's been too far long since I held your hand,' Will argued contrarily when he knew he should do exactly what she wanted him to and then walk away. 'Remember the part of our wedding vows where we said to have and to hold?' he drawled as if he was the same idle fool he was before he met her. What on earth had got into him now?

She had, of course—the vital fact of her, even so much thinner and paler than he remembered her. It was too much of a challenge not to spark back at her and he was supposed to be cool and aloof and disconnected from

the world, but how he wished he could turn
back the clock.

That was clearly impossible, so why *was*
he being so rude to the woman he had married and deserted? Because the changes in
her when he watched her get down from her
brother's carriage just now had shaken him
to the core. That neat, plainly dressed female
seemed so self-contained he had to look twice
to make sure she really was his bright Helena
more than six years on. This version of her had
been such a shock he nearly gave his feelings
away in front of Pensham, who only sent for
her to refute Will's ridiculous assertion they
were wed before he threw him out on his ear.

Will had backed away from the window
only just in time to avoid the quick survey
Lady Helena Snowe gave the grand façade of
her brother's lofty mansion before she ran up
the steps and headed inside with such breezy
certainty it made him quail for the blow he
was about to land her. He had to fight his in-
stinctive response to her, the one woman who
could take him to the heights and depths he
had never even known existed until they met.

He had told himself she was just a lady like

any other, but then he saw her again. His mind could rap sharp orders at his body not to respond to the mere sight of her as much as it liked, but he still could not turn and face her until he had it under control again. Now she looked a fraction less weary, a bit more eager for life under her quite understandable fury at him for his grievous lies and he knew he would disappoint her.

'Now, let me see—did that come before loving, comforting and cherishing until death did us part or afterwards, Captain?' she asked him loftily.

'If you cannot remember, I have no idea how you expect me to,' he said because he had to at least try to seem indifferent.

'But death has parted us for so very long,' she said and shifted in his hold so she could glare at him with poker-backed offence in every line of her body.

He wanted to kiss her so badly he was fighting for control again. Nothing was more likely to set him dancing about on the wrong end of Pensham's rapier early tomorrow morning but there was no time for all that.

'We can talk about it later,' he said with a

significant glance at her brother, but his gaze soon swung back to her face like a magnet to the north. She had been so lovely six and a half years ago and under the dull, spinster-in-waiting clothes she was pared down and even more breathtaking than the bold, untried young Her Ladyship.

My Helena—my bright unique love, the young idiot he'd once been sighed.

Go back to sleep, grown-up, realistic Will ordered him sharply.

'No, no,' she said implacably. 'There will be no later for us, just the lawyers.'

'Have I got a lovelorn swain to sue for criminal conversation with my wife?' he tried to joke, but waited for her answer with every nerve tensed.

'Of course not,' she said with such queenly dignity he was glad she was looking haughtily away from him so she didn't see relief and sheer grinding need in his eyes…but doubted he had managed to hide it from her brother.

'How dare you, Harborough?' Snowe blustered, but didn't seem as set on despising him as when he first realised why Will had come here—to admit he was alive and married to the man's only sister. 'I should call you out for that slur on my sister's honour as well as the fact you two married so secretly in the first place.'

'I am still officially dead so you can hardly fight a shadow,' Will said with an annoyed shrug. If only he wasn't so sick of bloodshed, maybe it would be the ideal way to make sure Helena never wanted anything to do with him again.

'As I do not have a lover and you are still alive, we cannot be rid of one another that easily so we will just have to stay married, whether we like it or not,' Helena told him as if she wished she *had* been unfaithful now it was too late.

'Just as well that I never want to be married to anyone else, then,' he told her truthfully, but of course she took it as another goad.

'What, not to a Spanish paramour or some woman you had with you in hiding?'

'I was in Spain for most of the time, but I was far too busy to woo any lovers at all.'

'So was I,' she said starkly.

'Check,' he whispered in her ear and longed to kiss it, then smooth back her richly curling mass of tawny hair and…

'Checkmate,' she argued haughtily, looking so magnificent he wondered if all the men in Gloucestershire were blind or daft not to have wooed her in droves while he was away.

'Not yet,' he replied, trying not to remember how heady it felt to spar and argue and refuse to concede dominance with her in the old days.

'Yes, yet,' she argued and shifted in his loosened embrace.

'I expect you need tea, Nell. I will ring for some,' Snowe barked with an anxious look at his sister's chalk-pale face.

'Don't you dare, I feel better now,' Helena argued.

'Of course you do,' Will murmured and shifted away from her because it was wrong to want her so badly when he had shaken her world to its very foundations.

'Don't presume that you know me, you lying, cheating, creeping along the ground worm!' she hissed with such venom he let her go. 'You don't know anything about me now,' she added, but didn't get to her feet to glare at him from a distance so she wasn't as fully recovered as she wanted them to think.

'I expect the full story now, Harborough,'

her brother warned softly and he saw how much the man had changed from the entitled young fribble who had threatened Will with a horsewhipping if he didn't leave his sister alone all those years ago.

He should have listened, but still traded this mature lord a long, cool look to say it was none of his business. 'I told you as much as it's safe for you to know,' he told him.

'You have given my brother the story behind all your shabby lies, but not me? You have played the lowest, *cruellest* trick on me and I am your wife, for goodness sake, so you owe me an explanation—always supposing you *can* explain such wicked callousness, which I doubt.'

'I had my reasons,' Will said flatly.

'Not good enough ones for what you did to me.'

It was wrong to feel passion grab him like a great fist as her grey eyes went stormy with fury. She finally stood up to stare down at him as if he was something unpleasant she had got on her shoe. The longing to settle this in bed, as they would have during their heady week of loving, felt so sharp he wanted it right now.

No, he must stay aloof and alert for her sake, that was the reminder he needed.

She gave her brother a weary smile that made Will want to rub his chest and soothe the ache of remembering her glorious smile of welcome whenever they met in secret before they were married. It was so hard for her to hide her feelings for him back then and Will suddenly longed for the absolute warmth and trust his loving, passionate, open-hearted lover of six and most of a half-year ago had given so generously. But he had killed her love and all that lovely trust and never mind if he had to kill idealistic young Will Harborough as well. He had done what had to be done to keep her safe.

'Then I am a rat with a nagging wife,' Will said, his jealousy of her strong bond with her brother rough in his voice.

'Don't even try to divert me with insults; I want to know why, Will. Why didn't you find some way to let me know you were alive? I suppose that lie did set you free to do what you wanted to behind my back,' she accused him and suddenly she began to cry as if that felt like the final straw.

He felt helpless and the wall he had built

round his emotions five years ago felt as if it was about to crack beyond repair. He knew he had hurt her beyond words because she would not cry for less. So, he watched five years of his lies run down her cheeks and how could he comfort her when he had caused every one? He had come here so determined not to feel again, but now he longed to be Lady Helena Snowe's passionate husband so stupidly it hurt. If that lie had never been told, he could tug her into his arms and soothe her tears with penitent, passionate kisses, but instead he had to watch his wife weep while he beat Will the Lover into submission.

She clenched her hands into fists as if she wanted to punch him and he just stared dumbly back and wished she would because that would hurt less. At last she turned her head away in disgust and he could not soothe or kiss her or tell her how badly he had missed her. In fact, he had done his best to forget all about Will Harborough while he pretended to be someone else and this was no time to thaw out a frozen heart. He was only here to make sure she stayed alive. That was all that mattered to him now.

Chapter Three

Helena longed for some time alone to work through this bolt from a blue sky without Will's sharp eyes watching her. Once upon a time he had set the stars in the sky for her, but he wasn't that man any more. It felt as if this older, harsher version of her wild young lover had done his best to kill her Will off. She squeezed her eyes shut against more tears because it was a shame to waste them on him. She opened them again to see him swap glares with Edward and knew they would fight if she let them.

'Look what you've done now, Harborough. Nell's crying and—' her brother said.

'I stopped nearly as soon as I started to, though, and at least I did not faint,' she cut him off before he could issue that challenge.

And she had only cried at all because her dashing young love was watching her like a grim stranger. Part of her still wanted to reach across the years, tangle her fingers with his again, find out if her Will was still in there somewhere. Maybe then she could let her senses say, *Yes, this is him, my husband and lover gloriously and miraculously alive.* Her heart could sing and dance and do the things young Helena wanted to, if he hadn't left her alone and grief-stricken for five years.

'And that proves you are a woman in a million,' Will said soothingly.

'Don't pacify me with more lies, Will Harborough. Right now I could kill you myself and make your biggest one of all come true,' she said furiously.

She refused to straighten her tumbling hair or hide her swollen eyes because this was a reality they both had to face. She was older and thinner and he was the man he had made himself into without her. He didn't look as if he had done a very good job with all that grey in his hair and such guarded eyes, but even now he could make her heart turn over with just a cynical smile. She felt the unfairness of what time and his lies had done to her when he was only more austerely handsome than her wild young lover and she felt less in every way than eager young Helena Harborough.

'You might have to stand in line,' he said with a shrug that said he was only half joking.

She wanted to scream, *Don't you dare let them kill you for real this time; I can't endure that cold hell any longer.* But Lady Helena Harborough had learned self-restraint in a hard school. The idea of someone shooting him or slipping a knife between his ribs one dark night hurt so much she knew she still loved him. But he didn't need to know that.

'Aye, behind me for one,' Edward said grimly and the challenge both men were longing to throw at one another was prickly in the air between them once again. As soon as the words were out their mouthes neither of the stubborn idiots would lower themselves to take them back.

'I would rather you did not kill my husband, thank you, Ed,' she told him sternly.

'Just name your seconds and get it over with, then, Pensham,' Will argued as if she hadn't spoken so she glared at him instead.

'You are *not* fighting one another and that's final,' she told them furiously. 'I will *not* let you goad my brother into challenging you to a duel because you think it is easier than trying to explain yourself to me. Instead you can tell me where you have been all these years and why the *devil* you pretended to be dead.'

'I told you, I was busy in Spain for most of them,' he said curtly and ignored the second part of her question, as if he thought she would stop asking it if he evaded it deftly enough.

'Busy?'

'Yes, and when I was done there, I had to wait for the right moment to come back to life.'

'Busy, as in your ship was kept in port by a choppy sea, or busy as in you waited years for your horse to be reshod, or for your fingers to recover the ability to write to your own wife? Or were you *busy* as in there were far more seductive reasons than me to be quite happy pretending you were dead while I mourned you in secret?'

Drat, now she had given her almost unbearable grief away along with her stinging jealousy of the women he must have bedded while she felt hardly even half alive without him. It might salve her pride if he was busy imagining half the single men in the area competing for her attention until she had all but forgotten him as well. But he was hardly going to do that when missing him had robbed her of her bloom and she looked old and worn and he had already accused her of being skinny.

'I was never happy about the pretence,' he told her with a hunted look.

'Then why do it?' she challenged again. For some self-torturing reason she wanted to know every lover he had taken since he'd left her bed. A glimpse of genuine regret in his eyes argued it would be little and petty and give too much away if she demanded a list of them in front of her brother.

'*I* didn't put my name on the list of dead,' Will said as if that excused him of any responsibility for it being there.

'Yet somehow it still got there. I heard the news of your death in battle at a soirée. It was whispered in my ear between a snatch of Bach and a happy little trill of Mozart. That was how I learned my husband was dead—from one of the worst gossips of the *ton* who must

have been in the confidence of someone in-
discreet at the War Office to know before anyone else.

'Then I had to sit there and pretend you
were an old flirt I had all but forgotten about,
since you swore me to secrecy unless I was
with child and I was not. I said I was very
sorry Captain Harborough was dead, but I
had not seen you for a year and a half and my
family did not approve of you. I knew she
wanted me to be broken, but she scurried off
to whisper how hard-hearted I was instead,
so at least she was happy. It hardly mattered
what she said because inside I felt as if I had
died as well.'

'Shock,' Edward said abruptly and began to
pace the room. At least he cared for her pain
and grief in hindsight, even if Will didn't.

That report of his death had made it so
difficult to bluff her way through the Little
Season with a broken heart that it had felt
impossible to tell her brother the truth and
at least she had always had Kate's sympathy
and support.

'Did you ever truly love me, Will?' she said
bleakly because he was not dead and now she

had to feel guilty because Kate's Sir Kester really was and Will's re-emergence changed everything about Helena's life from now on.

'Of course I did,' he replied, but the past tense stung like a whip.

'How I itch for my Mantons, Harborough,' her brother warned him.

'Nothing is solved by violence,' she told them both sternly.

'But I would feel so much better about sending for you so he could treat you like this if I could take a few pot-shots at him,' Edward argued half seriously.

'I would not be much loss,' Will said with a weary shrug that made her ache for the vital young rogue of six and a half years ago and for young, besotted Helena Snowe.

'Be quiet, you; I have spent so many years mourning you in secret I won't let you throw your life away now,' she snapped.

'I really did love you,' Will said with a hunted glance at the window, as if he would rather be out there than in here telling even more lies.

'Not enough to tell me the truth,' she said flatly and he didn't argue. 'You look like my

Will would if someone had left him out in the rain for a decade or two, but you certainly don't act like him.'

'That Will Harborough is truly dead and good riddance,' he said.

And she wanted to shout, *No! He can't be; I loved him with all my heart!* But she didn't.

'I should never have married you in such a hole-and-corner fashion.'

'For that *I* shall challenge you to a duel and may the best spouse win,' she told him because temper felt good. It was hot and invigorating and richly deserved and stopped her hurting so savagely she wanted to curl up into a ball and rock herself to sleep. Then maybe she could forget the hurt and betrayal fighting with this girlish joy dancing inside her simply because he was alive. That girl only cared that he was a breathing, living being. She had spent so many years longing for even one more minute with him, how could she truly wish this strangeness and confusion gone and him still dead?

Yet all you have in common now is a wedding ring, she told herself fiercely, and clenched her fists when she saw not even a pale band on his left hand to say he had worn his recently. She was sure he wouldn't have kept his on a chain like the one suddenly so heavy round her neck either.

'I meant it was wrong of me to marry you and go back to war.'

'Our marriage was wrong, or you going away as if you hardly knew me was wrong?'

'The war—I couldn't bed you without offering marriage,' he murmured with a hunted look at Edward.

Perhaps Will only ever wanted her, then. He certainly didn't look as if he did now that she was old and worn and skinny, but he was hard-edged and remote and aged beyond his years as well. And she still wanted him as if a thousand hungry devils inside her were crying out for his sinful attentions. Her knees were so weak with it she tightened her fists until her nails dug into her palms and maybe the pain would kill this stupid wanting as stone dead as his feelings for her. 'Were our wedding and honeymoon merely expedient?' she asked stiffly.

'I take it your rash marriage cannot be annulled?' Edward barked as if he had been pinning his hopes on one to free her from her youthful folly.

'Of course not,' she said impatiently. Denying the passion that had burned between her and Will once upon a time would make those driven young lovers a lie as well and she could not do it to them.

'No,' Will agreed, so at least he had that much truth in him.

'Then I have the perfect cure for your youthful mistake,' Edward said grimly and she was torn between fear and fury at the stubborn pigheadedness of men.

'You are *not* going to shoot him and *you* know perfectly well he cannot shoot you since it's my honour you claim to want to fight over. *I* have the right not to be fought over like a juicy bone and *you* are about to become a father, Edward Snowe, and should know better. Mattie will be left to raise your child alone if you kill my husband in a duel, or would you prefer her and the babe to trail around the Continent after you as you flee charges of fratricide?'

'He's not my brother,' Edward insisted with a morose glower.

'You know perfectly well he became one to you by law when I married him.'

'I could always disown you before I shot him,' he said with a wistful glare at Will to say he was probably joking.

'And I refuse to lose either of you to a so-called matter of honour. Now, please go away and leave us to sort this mess out between us, Ed,' she pleaded.

'If that's what *you* want, I suppose I must,' Edward said and started to pace the room again. He glanced out of Will's window. 'Oh, damnation, here's the gig racing down the hill with Mama in a fine pother!' he exclaimed.

'She will fall into strong hysterics the moment she sees Will and goodness knows what she will do when she finds out I have been married to him while she was so desperate to marry me off,' Helena said glumly.

Edward looked torn between his masculine longing to escape a scene and the need to protect his sister. 'Sneak away before she gets here, then, Nell. Take him up Blundell Hill and I will come and meet you up there as soon as I can get away,' he said with a long-suffering sigh.

'None of this must come out until I finally scotch the snake on my tail, Pensham,' Will warned before he would give in to Helena's urgent tug on his resistant hand so she could lead him out of here before her mother found out what she was missing.

'Best hurry away unless you want the world to know you are alive, then, Harborough; my mother is almost at the door.'

'Brave of you, Ed,' Helena said with a quick hug for her brother as she heard the Dowager make a fine fuss even as the gig drew to a halt. 'Come *on*,' she said and tugged even harder on Will's hand.

Chapter Four

'Hurry,' Helena urged and since Will didn't want to meet her mother again either he decided he might as well. They were outside in a matter of seconds and fleeing the place as if the devil was on their heels. He loped along in her wake and frowned as she hesitated at a fork in the path as if she had almost forgotten the way.

'We'll be caught in the act of running away if we don't hurry,' he prompted.

'You are good at running from the Snowe family, but it's a novelty for me,' she snapped, but at least she seemed to have remembered exactly where she was.

'I did not run away from you,' he said, sounding like a sulky schoolboy.

'No, you marched—that made all the difference.'

'Later,' he said curtly. He could hear the Dowager Countess working herself into a state even from out here. 'Your brother is a brave man,' he muttered.

'Yes, only think what he is enduring right now so you don't have to.'

'He is a true gentleman,' he said and held on to his temper with both hands.

'Yes, he is, isn't he?'

'And unless you want his noble sacrifice to be wasted, we need to get on with that running away you mentioned.'

'Indeed,' she said coolly, but tugged him on to the right-hand path after a hunted glance behind her to see if they had been spotted from the house.

Thank goodness she was too intent on scurrying him away to break their contact, even if her touch was making it devilish hard to concentrate. Her hand in his woke so many feelings he had been trying to forget since he walked away from her all those years ago. Now they were skin to skin again, all those old wild wants and deep feelings were coming tumbling back to him and it was almost painful, as if blood was rushing into a cramped limb or a half-healed wound.

'Now you can tell me why,' she said when they reached the cover of a broad old oak tree with branches sweeping nearly all the way to the ground.

'Not here,' he said with a nod to the house and all the windows they might still be seen from if her mother looked hard enough for her errant daughter.

'You are impossible,' she said sharply.

'And right.'

'The odds say even you have to be once in a while,' she said. 'Oh, very well; I don't want to be interrupted either,' she admitted with a heavy sigh.

He tried not to smile as she tugged him away from their temporary refuge. Her fury felt better than those tears or having to watch her almost faint with shock as the true depth of his lie sank in. He felt a little less like the worm she likened him to now her truly beautiful grey eyes were sparkling with intriguing depths and silver flecks again.

Even as the acknowledged beauty he had

first met she had never seemed to realise what a magnificent female she was, so he would have his work cut out proving it to her with all their years apart stark in her memory. But that wasn't what he was here for, was it? He was not a simple soldier back from the wars against all odds and she was not a simple wife, content with a tall story and an eager husband in her bed.

At least scurrying away from her brother's grand mansion had put colour back in her cheeks and he should be watching where they were going, looking for anyone trying to follow even in the very heart of Snowe's power, but he was too fascinated by his wife to take his eyes off her long enough. She had always made him blind to any other female.

Now his eyes and thoughts were all bound up in her again, as if he was put under an enchantment years ago and nothing would shake it. However dangerous it felt, he might as well get this Helena settled in his mind so he could be more use at keeping her safe.

The last of her youthful softness had gone and that was probably his fault. The fining down of the privileged young woman she'd once been only made her features more starkly elegant and her eyes seem even larger and lovelier. Her mouth was always fascinating, and it had not changed even when she tried to purse it as if he had no right to read anything of her feelings and now her teeth were worrying at her lower lip to remind him how sweet and luscious it tasted when he had kissed and licked and caressed it as her lusty and lust-driven husband far too long ago.

This was not what he was here for, though. She was glaring at him as if she could read his wicked desires as plainly as if he had shouted them out loud so he shot her a *What?* look to pretend he was innocent of needing her as fiercely as ever. But of course he was lying.

He had outfaced some of the worst brigands in Spain during his time there. He had lied through his teeth and looked them straight in the eye as if he was the soul of truth, but he had to look away from his wife's accusing ones and his gaze rested on her mouth instead and now his inner idiot wanted to kiss her even more urgently. Despite her chilly gaze, and the punishing pace she was setting, she had so nearly fainted only minutes ago, but that tender mouth of hers gave her away. It trembled when he gazed at it like a starving beggar.

She firmed it to pretend she was coldly resolute and he might as well go away again, but he had seen that giveaway wobble and the way she nibbled at her now reddened lower lip to say she was nowhere near as cold about his stupid male wants as she was trying to pretend.

Don't get your hopes up, Will the Lover, he tried to tell his old self.

But the illusion was wearing thin. A sidelong glance caught her licking that delicious lower lip and he knew she was more upset than she wanted him to know. Even worse, when she parted her lips to catch her breath he remembered how it felt to make love to her time after memorable, driven, time during their brief honeymoon. He had forgotten to notice where they were going again now and what sort of protector did that make him?

A useless one, he decided. He must stop fantasising about making love to his wife and sharpen his senses on the world around them. He needed to know if hostile eyes were on them and at least he could see and sense nothing more threatening than a squirrel's exasperated chatter and a kestrel hovering for prey in the distance, but it was far too hard to concentrate with Helena dominating those senses.

This was not the time to recall a younger Helena so full of love and trust and all the other glorious things he never deserved. She had been so sweetly, unashamedly sensual the first time they made love and every moment of their honeymoon they could cram more loving into. And it was such a very long time since he could explore her smart, sensual mouth with hot kisses. He longed to explore the differences and revel in the blissful familiarity of her delicious body and quirky, eager mind, but he had no right to do so. Not after what he had done. She would not give him permission for a glorious sensual exploration of them as mature lovers yet and maybe never again.

So, what about him? Most people would set him the wrong side of forty instead of not quite thirty years old. Better men must have tried to catch his wife's eye since he left her behind and jealousy slammed into him like a fist and warned him the old, impulsive Will was fighting his way through the barriers he had tried to hold him back with.

Not allowed, he mouthed at his younger self, then glanced at Helena to see if she had noticed. Luckily, she was looking the other way and he was glad she was leading the way so he could focus on hating every male who had set eyes on her these last six and a half years. Yet having her walk ahead of him also meant getting too good a view of her slender hips and glorious feminine legs moving so fast he wondered if she was trying to lose him in grounds she must know well.

He made himself speed up to thwart her if she was, but could not take his eyes off her thin summer skirts, clinging to her legs as she stormed up the slope, and he bit back a groan. Ordering his rampant sex to stand down and behave itself, he gritted his teeth.

Ice houses and frozen wastes and you still have a devil stalking you, he reminded himself as he tried to watch his feet instead of hers.

It was much too hard to listen for any small giveaway human noises to warn that they were being followed. All his ears wanted to hear was the swish of Lady Helena's thinnest of lawn and lace petticoats and her airy muslin gown against her slender legs. At first glance, he had thought her grey muslin sadly shabby and wrong for his bright Helena. Now it looked insubstantial as autumn mist and made a delicious, diaphanous foil for her multi-hued hair.

He certainly wasn't going to point out it had slipped most of its pins and was tumbling halfway down her back. He could never decide if it was red or brown or honeyed amber, but realised now that it was all three and as fiery and subtle and tempting as the lady herself, but this would not do.

This was no lover's tryst; they were not heading towards the glory his little man was so eager for. He owed her more than a tumble in the hay after all those lies, even if she would let him have his very wicked way with her. His Helena had always felt more, thought more deeply and expected more than he had taught himself to. Except the lies he told himself about forgetting her for her own good were only that, as his fascination with her every move and gesture proved now. He had not forgotten a hair or a whisper of hers, but he should still have resisted the absolute temptation of her headlong desire for all they could be together and walked away with only a promise to marry her if he survived the war.

He made himself look away from her hurrying figure and realised they were already on the other side of the hill and looking into a shallower valley. Despite all those years of nerve-tingling wariness, he had not even noticed the August sun hot on his back until she paused to watch him warily. He shot the green bowl of land a quick look and tried to concentrate on the menace on his tail. What was he thinking of to be so unwary for a moment, let alone so many?

Best not answer that, Harborough, he chided himself and tried to make up for his negligence while she stared at him as if she wasn't quite sure who he was either.

'My grandparents liked to pretend they were simpler folk now and again,' she explained as if he was an acquaintance on a duty tour of her brother's park. 'This is as private as we are likely to be and at least my brother's tenants and labourers are busy with the harvest.' She nodded at the faux cottage and took the path down to it before he could argue. 'Are you going to tell me why you are here, Will? Please don't pretend there's nothing more to your reappearance than a belated need to tell me the truth,' she challenged as soon as they got there.

He winced at her bitter words and it felt dangerous to hope one day intimacy could build bridges between them better than words.

'Well?' she said impatiently. 'Are you ever going to answer me, or shall we sit in yonder folly glaring at one another until sunset?'

He turned away to hide a smile and when he looked again she stared warily back as if she didn't trust him an inch. She was right not to; he had to look over her shoulder to get his stupid body into that imaginary ice house again and once he could actually see what he was looking at, instead of wondering what her pared-down curves looked like without those airy, misty draperies, he took a proper look at the imitation cottage nestled into the hillside and ordered his brain to work.

'Best sit out here,' he said in a strangled voice, 'you'll be warmer.'

'I am hardly likely to catch a chill on a day

like this,' she said, but looked almost as overheated by her hasty march here as he felt.

Awareness of her every move was bad enough out here, but take him inside her grandparents' romantic hideaway and Helena would be unsafe for a very different reason from the one that brought him here. A fantasy of her willing and responsive in his arms once again, warming him as he hadn't felt warm since he last left her bed, shot straight to his sex and he had to turn away from the sight of her flushed and ruffled by their walk. If he wasn't careful, she would realise why he was so husky and clumsy and hate him for it.

'Is anyone likely to follow us and try to eavesdrop?' he asked as casually as he could when he was desperate to know if she had a suitor or, God forbid, a lover despite her hot denials in front of her brother.

'I don't know—did you bring any enemies with you?' she asked with too many questions in her sharply intelligent eyes.

'Not yet,' he said before he could guard his tongue.

Her eyes widened as she realised she had

hit the mark without trying. 'Who is he, then?' she demanded.

'I don't know,' he said with a wanting-to-be-careless shrug he suspected she did not believe in for one moment.

'You have offended so many people you don't know which one to worry about the most?'

'Yes.'

'Captain Popular,' she accused him with a wry smile he wanted to kiss off her lips even more than he had when she'd refused to smile at him earlier.

'Not exactly and it would be Major Popular, if I hadn't sold out,' he said with a rueful shrug.

'Maybe you should have stayed dead, then, Major.'

'Better for you if I had,' he said and her silver-grey eyes clouded, then sharpened on his until he found her gaze too hard to meet.

'You must have pretended to be dead for a reason. I do hope she was worth it,' she said, staring at a row of elm trees as if she couldn't look at him any longer.

'I suppose you are entitled to an explanation,' he said and an edited version of the truth might stop her digging any deeper.

'I am, Major.' She sounded hurt and wary, yet there was something else in her voice he could not quite put his finger on.

Don't think about fingers or touch or the feel of warm woman under them or, even better, the feel of your warm and responsive wife.

His once warm and responsive wife, the one he had lied to and left bereft and alone. Where was he? Ah, yes, lies and half-truths—he was good at those.

'In material terms, I am a much better bet than I was six years ago,' he said clumsily.

He might as well work up to half-truths, except the faint noise of her foot tapping impatiently on the stone terrace said he wasn't very good at them either. Where was the wily spy who had rooted out so many truths people didn't want him to know about when he needed him?

'When I first became a soldier, I had a big cousin and another uncle and a father between me and the family earldom, but Lord Flamington and I are the only two Harboroughs left now. Uncle Peter…he insists on giving me a more than generous allowance as his heir, although I don't really need it now I am past five and twenty and can inherit my great-grandmother's house and family estate outright.'

'I hope you and your uncle are not expecting me to become a brood mare for your endangered line,' Helena said distantly.

It stung all the harder because he could think of nothing finer than watching her grow big with his child and he wasn't even sure if she would let him back in her bed to make one yet. 'You married me when I had no hope of a title and you brought far more to our marriage than I did,' he told her as if that explained his latest piece of clumsiness.

'That was then; now I shall happily wear this gown until it falls apart rather than ask you for a penny,' she said as if she meant it.

'I have made sure you will be comfortably off if anything happens to me this time,' he said and there it was again—clumsiness.

He saw shock widen her eyes again. 'This time?' she echoed at last.

'I was a spy, Helena,' he made himself say because he couldn't tell her more lies and expect her to believe them now; he wasn't a good enough liar with her.

'Ah, I see,' she said after a long and very thoughtful look at his face, which was supposed to be inscrutable. 'There was always something secretive about your insistence on keeping our marriage quiet unless I was with child. I should have suspected it, but I was too blindly in love to see how odd that was.'

'Even I am not quite as much of a rogue that I would wed you when I could be unmasked and shamed at any moment.'

'Yet you have been married to me all this time and it doesn't appear to have stopped you.'

'I had to; circumstances forced it on me,' he said and groaned as he felt her put the worst interpretation on his words. Why couldn't his mind untangle itself before his tongue got him into trouble? 'I mean the spying, not our wedding.'

'Oh, good, how nice to know you embraced our marriage almost voluntarily.'

'I did.'

'Did you? I wonder.'

'I loved you.'

'I doubt it,' she said stonily and he had a mountain to climb, but he looked back over those years and decided he deserved it.

'I shall have to convince you I really was in love with you, then.'

'That was then and if you ever truly *loved* me, you clearly don't *love* me now—different tenses, you see, Will?'

'A slip of the tongue.'

'A slip that tells the truth and I prefer it to the lie you are trying to tell now.'

'It's not a lie. I have never loved any other woman but you and I didn't have a string of mistresses either.'

'Congratulations on your sturdy campaign against all those eager Spanish beauties we wives have heard so much about.'

Chapter Five

Will cursed his jangling emotions and stupid male pride while he had tried to pretend he wasn't bowled over by his own wife earlier. He didn't want to be in love with her again when he had an assassin stalking him; he might be so absorbed in loving her he left them open to the very threat he had come here to frustrate.

'Did you marry me for money, Will? What a poor bargain you got if so.'

'Of course not.' He was shocked how much her accusation hurt. 'I loved you.'

'Then you marched away, pretended you were dead and became a spy, so of course I can see how deeply you cared for me,' she said bitterly.

He *had* married her because he loved her and because he was so blind and deaf to all the reasons he should not when he could not stop himself making love to her. 'I was a crass fool to even think I could be an observing officer after I married you, Helena, but that was my folly, not marrying you in the first place. I should have sold out or stayed on as an ordinary officer and let you come with me.'

'*Let* me? I have never wanted to be a *duty* to my husband and I don't now.'

'You are my wife; I made solemn promises I failed to keep, although you must admit you did everything you could to persuade me to take you with me, short of stowing away in my luggage.'

'The difference between us being that I listened in the end; I heard your reason for leaving me behind safe in England and honoured it, although I didn't want to. I could see how the retreat through Spain and the fighting and chaos and brutality at Corunna damaged you. I deferred to your rasped feelings instead of following my own desire to be with you in any way I could get there. You can have no idea how terrified I was every time there was a report of a battle or skirmishes in the newssheets and I had to search for your name among the dead and wounded without anyone realising it.

'You didn't think about me at Snowe House or back here worrying about you and pining for you in secret when you let yourself be declared dead and were clearly nothing of the sort.' She paused and took a deep breath, shot him a hard, wifely glare as if she was remembering all the things he should have done after they were married and did not. 'So never mind your guilty conscience, I survived without you and dare say I can do so again,' she said, removing her hand from his as if his touch was poison to her.

He felt so cold without her warmth. Her touch had made him think he could be fully alive again for a heady moment. But he had no right to feed off her finer emotions when his were locked away. He shoved his hands into his pockets to stop them seeking hers again although it felt as if he was wilfully throwing away true happiness a second time. 'I meant to honour all my vows, not just the cleaving only unto you ones,' he said ruefully and she looked unconvinced.

'I am not a set of promises you made when

you were too young to know better, Will. Or if I am, we had best part until one of us really does die and sets the other one free,' she told him distantly.

His heart missed a beat, then raced on as if galloping at Newmarket because the idea of the rest of his life without her was intolerable. He could hardly recognise the cynical fool who came here so determined to warn her and Pensham of the danger stalking him, then walk away so he could draw it with him. 'I will never give up on them, even if you do,' he said—where had that come from?

'Then tell me why you are here now and why you didn't tell me you were alive after Bussaco. Spies can do things we ordinary mortals cannot so I know you could have found a way to get a message to me if you really wanted to.'

'It was safer if we seemed completely unconnected after a brief flirtation,' he said and saw her mouth tighten again. 'I am truly sorry you had to hear about my supposed death from the gossips,' he said stiffly. However she felt about him now, she had loved him when they'd wed. He had not allowed himself to see the full cruelty of what he agreed to do to her when he agreed to that false tale until now.

'So am I. I had to pretend it was only a summer cold that ailed me when I felt so broken inside,' she said bleakly.

He should be on his knees begging her forgiveness.

'I am so sorry, Helena,' he said inadequately instead.

'Oh, good, Captain—no, Major—Harborough is sorry. That makes everything right again, then, doesn't it?'

'I very much doubt it.'

'No, it makes it about as not right as it is possible to be.'

'I can see that,' he said, but it only made things worse.

'You wish you were free of me, don't you?'

'No, that's not true. *I* am no use to you as a lover or husband, not the other way around,' he burst out. She still looked so bleakly self-contained he wanted to weep for her and maybe himself as well. 'I cannot sleep peacefully through the night and hate travelling in a closed carriage or living at close quarters with anyone. I have been more like a hunted and hunting animal than a man for so long I should have stayed dead and left you in peace for all the use I am to you now.'

'When did you truly come home, Will?' she asked with a challenging look to say, *Lie to me again if you dare.*

'I came back to England briefly before being recalled to my grubby spying duties when Bonaparte left Elba this spring.'

'I won't ask why you didn't come and find me then, but the war was supposed to have been over this April twelvemonth so what were you doing in between the Armistice and March this year?'

'I have been the Duke's secret liaison officer,' he finally admitted, 'and I was working to try to unite various bands of Spanish guerrillas until Wellington went over the Pyrenees and into France. Apparently, I was the only man he could trust to pass himself off as a Spaniard and report back the truth to him, but it was hard to convince them I was trustworthy at times. There were so many factions and contrary interests at work, even while they struggled for their freedom, that I suppose I can hardly blame them.'

'Oh, Will. Even I know how barbaric the guerrillas' struggle with the French was and how badly they suffered for rebelling against their so-called King, Joseph Bonaparte. You must have seen some appalling sights if you spent much time with them.'

'Their country was being torn apart and it was left savaged and abandoned when the British and the French left Spain. It will take decades for the Spanish people to live anything like a normal life again,' he told her. Thinking of all their opposing factions and deep grudges made him grieve for his Spanish grandmother's beloved homeland all over again. 'I knew I should come home as soon as my secret duty was done there and my masters had plenty of fluent French speakers at their disposal to take over my secretive role. But since I was pretending to be a half-blooded Spanish rogue who could obtain impossible things for the right price during the war, I stayed on to try to get some to the people who truly needed them.'

'I should be glad I never knew about the dangers you faced in Spain and when Napoleon was welcomed back to France this spring.

I would have gone white with worry if I knew you were alive and taking so many risks,' she said.

Was there a glimmer of hope for him behind that shaken admission?

'That would be a crying shame so it's as well I did so instead,' he joked with a casual wave at his once sooty locks and a hungry one at her richly tawny-coloured ones.

'You suffered with your Spanish grand-mother's people, didn't you?' she said and put a hand out as if she was going to touch his greying hair and maybe even test the feel of it against her memories. He longed for even her fleeting touch like a smitten idiot, but she snatched her hand back. How stupid to yearn for contact she could not bring herself to make.

'All I did was skulk in corners and pretend to be someone else,' he said, sounding harsher than he intended because he was disappointed and why would she touch him when he didn't deserve it? '*I* didn't suffer, Helena,' he went on. 'The Spanish people suffered; soldiers on either side suffered disease and hardship, appalling injury and death, but I hid in dark corners with the other vermin.'

'I know you better and this says you lie,' she said with a wave at the grey among his sooty curls. He wished he had dyed them to disguise it now.

'I had an easy enough time of it,' he said with a trying-to-be-careless shrug.

'Don't treat me like a silly widgeon with more hair than sense because you think I am too fragile to endure the truth. I know better and you won't fool me again, Will, so please stop trying.'

'Let's just say I got used to being powerless to stop any of it. All I could do for Spain was hope Wellington could drag the war over the Pyrenees and into France as soon as possible and leave her to lick her wounds and bury the dead.'

Helena eyed Will's averted face and knew how much the war had hurt him despite his efforts to shrug it off. Now she knew *her* Will was in there somewhere, behind the shuttered gaze and touch-me-not air and cynicism. And, yes, it *was* hard to be on the outside of his defences but at least he was here and that was so much better than the aching void living without him had made of her life. Maybe loss had taught her more patience than he deserved because she could wait for more now; hope for a very different future than the one she had been planning with Kate.

And that reminded her—she had to get a message to Kate and tell her things had changed so radically she would not be able to come and help her after all. She should be thinking of ways to make her best friend's life better without her help, but she could not keep her attention away from Will. Part of her didn't quite believe he was real yet. Maybe if she could touch him properly, explore all the differences between then and now in intimate detail she might truly believe she would not wake up in a while and feel more bereft and lonely than ever because of this incredible dream.

'Does anyone else know you are here, Major?' she asked in case she needed to worry about his safety even now.

'Maybe,' he said tersely.

'And they bear you a grudge?' she asked

and he hesitated. 'I only want the truth from this moment on so never mind my delicate feminine sensibilities; I never had many anyway.'

'Yes, you did, but my uncle has informed the War Office I survived the campaign in the Low Countries as well as all the others they never wanted to admit I was involved in. News I have been alive all along will soon leak since they were never good at keeping secrets even when we were still at war. So, yes, my enemies might remember me and take pot shots at me and save your brother the trouble.'

'Don't joke about it; you know he didn't mean it.'

'If I hurt you even a little more, he will issue that invitation to eat grass before breakfast the moment he tracks me down again.'

'Not if he ever wants me to speak to him again, he will not,' she said.

'But you two are close; I can tell how much he hates the pain and grief I inflicted on you in secret. There will be a fine scandal when my deception comes out and news of our secret marriage will add fuel to the fire.'

'It will be a nine-day wonder and what does

it matter to us anyway? I avoid high society nowadays and doubt you would like it very much after seeing so much of the real world these last few years.'

'True, but my Uncle Peter is a sociable man and one day I might have to be an earl in my turn, whether I want to or not,' he said as if he doubted it. Helena shuddered, because the only alternative now was for him to die before his uncle and she didn't like the sound of it at all.

'Why didn't you find me straight after Waterloo, Will?' she asked, because she suspected the secretive game he had played so long might not be over yet and he was still refusing to tell her why he'd lied. At heart, he was too honourable to have done such a monstrous thing without a good reason and logic whispered that reason could be that he was still running as he had not shouted his survival from the rooftops once Emperor Napoleon abdicated for the first time in April last year.

Will looked away again, as if searching for the right words to deflect her. 'Uncle Peter was so set on me providing him with some heirs at the double I didn't want you to feel like that brood mare you mentioned just now,' he said as if he thought she would hate the idea of bearing his children.

'Indeed?' she said coolly, although even the idea of them warmed a cold corner of her heart.

'I had to tell him about you when he was ready to invite every unwed female in the county to Deepdale to see if one of them could endure me as a husband.'

Endure? Most of the unattached young ladies in the West Country would leap at the chance to wed a man of his birth, broodingly handsome looks and glittering prospects. 'Well, you can hardly blame him for wanting you home and properly settled after believing he had lost you,' she said with a shrug.

'No, but I needed to prepare the ground and protect everyone's backs before I told the truth, then Bonaparte escaped from Elba so there was no point in me letting you know I was still alive when I might not be if I was caught behind enemy lines with my not quite so fluent French.'

How reckless of him to answer a recall to arms when so much depended on him staying alive here, but she still refused to be de-flected. 'Whose backs did you need to protect so badly you could not tell me you were still alive last year or this spring?' she demanded.

'Yours, Uncle Peter's, everyone I care about,' Will admitted reluctantly.

'You mean…?' She let her voice trail off as a look of desperation in his dark eyes said he was still in danger and believed she was, too.

'I mean you are in danger. I played dead for so long to make sure nobody could hurt you and make me suffer by proxy, but now the war is over and the powers-that-be feel no need to hide my continued existence any more. My se-crets are already seeping out and Uncle Peter thinks he has a dynasty to build.'

He sounded so bitter and anguished she wanted to push herself into his arms again and make him forget the terror stark in his eyes and never mind all the lost years between them. 'You agreed to that terrible lie to keep *us* safe?'

'My mother was murdered, Helena,' he said bleakly, as if that explained everything. But it didn't. Supported by her noble family when she left the husband they never approved of because he was a serving soldier and only the third son of an earl, the Lady Aurelia Harborough was murdered in her luxurious boudoir far away from her only child so why did he think her violent death was a good enough reason for doing what he had done? 'She was foully done away with and I received a threat saying that she was only the start of the rough justice I was about to receive.'

'Your mother's death had nothing to do with you.'

'My enemy has a long reach,' he insisted.

'The magistrates at Bow Street concluded one of her discarded lovers killed her in a jealous rage, although they never accused a particular man. I suppose if his family agreed to have him safely locked away, deference for his rank could account for their silence on that front.'

'And there were enough of her lovers to make tracking him down a challenge. If only that was what happened.'

Will's parents had abandoned him to his paternal relatives as a babe in arms and went their separate ways. Why anyone would murder his mother to hurt him was beyond her although he had a very soft heart under his cynical exterior so maybe that was it. The death of an ageing beauty so desperate to prove she was not losing her looks that she took lover after lover would hit Will hard, even if Lady Aurelia hardly deserved it to.

'Why are you convinced her death was *not* the crime of passion they were so adamant it was at the time?' she asked him.

'Because I might as well have stuck the knife in her myself,' he said starkly.

'From all those miles away?'

'Yes, she died because I had uncovered a traitor.'

'If you let him escape, I expect he was far more concerned with remaining at large than attacking your relatives to get back at you.'

'He didn't escape, Helena. The man was quietly shot, then declared dead in the next battle…and all well before my mother was murdered.'

'Such a convenient way for somebody to dispose of him,' she said. 'How could this traitor of yours be responsible for your mother's death when he was already dead, though?'

'He must have a lover or brother or father or

mother intent on revenge because one of them uncovered what really happened and knew I had exposed his treachery. I don't know how they found out I was the one who had stumbled on his meeting with the Frenchman the cur was selling arms and information to while I was still acting as an observing officer. That was as far as I was prepared to go to use my command of my grandmother's language until I grabbed that particular tiger by the tail and had to go further to protect you and everyone else I ever cared for.'

Hmm, Will having to go deeper into that harsh game to ferret out secrets his language skills equipped him so well for was a boon for his commanders, wasn't it? From her side of the story, Helena thought this needed thinking about when she wasn't so busy with uncovering Will's reasons for doing what he did to her.

'If someone shared his treachery, maybe they were doing their best to stop you looking any further. How many people knew you were the one who discovered his duplicity Will?'

'I only told the man who became my secret contact with Wellington and the great man himself when I became his spy and I would have sworn both of them are close as oysters.'

'Even so, I doubt the Duke went about the countryside shooting his own men, so who killed your traitor for him?'

'I have always supposed it was the friend who became my spymaster, but maybe someone saw him do it and told this tiger of mine, or maybe it was the tiger himself watching from the shadows,' Will said, making it clear he trusted his friend completely.

Yet the man had pitch-forked Will into a dangerous secret life that must have given this so-called friend an edge even in his secretive dealings with his commander-in-chief. Helena had to wonder if his friend had acted as selflessly as Will clearly thought he had. She also wondered how far had this mysterious friend of his progressed on the back of Will's efforts. She ordered herself not to be such a cynic since he believed in the friendship that had seen him through such dangerous times yet her distrust of the man's motives refused to go away.

'Even if someone saw, how could they know you were the one who caught the traitor?'

'I don't know, maybe Gr...' His voice tailed off as he realised he had nearly let out the name of the man who had run his life for so long. It hurt to know Will did not trust her with the man's name. She had proved she would keep his secrets when she stayed silent about their marriage when it happened and ever since. 'My contact and the Duke are so close-mouthed I would stake my life on their discretion. Indeed, I have done so for the last five years,' Will added.

'Maybe someone did overhear or see something of the man's true death,' she allowed, as if she might be convinced that was how it had happened. 'I suppose whoever wanted to know *could* have guessed you were the one who spied his comrade plying his dirty trade from afar. I know observing officers go wherever they can get away with going without being caught by the enemy so please don't try to convince me you were not already in danger, even before you put yourself in so much more as a spy without even a uniform to protect you if you were caught.'

'Never mind all that, it was a desperate and

dirty business. I didn't want you involved in it then and I don't now.'

'Don't treat me as a weak little woman you must guard from every harsh wind that blows, Will. Look what doing that did to us last time. This time I must feel what you feel, face what you face. I have a right to know it all after what you put me through these last five years and never mind my ladylike sensibilities.'

'I still don't know who this tiger is, Helena. You have no idea how hard it is to track down such a will-o'-the-wisp,' he said with a despairing shake of his head.

'And you have no idea how it feels to endure five years without hope,' she said fiercely, because despair was no longer an option for either of them.

Somehow, she would fight a secret foe he seemed to believe in so deeply he could not see the wood for trees. She would find a path out of that wood because now he was miraculously restored to life, they both had a future to fight for. She could not endure the idea of living under the same shadow that had all but snuffed out Will's hopes and dreams for the rest of their lives.

'That wasn't what you said just now,' he said with a wry smile, as if he could not quite believe he was her hope restored even now they were together again.

'I was angry with you; I still am,' she admitted and supposed it was partly her fault he didn't think he mattered to her as essentially as he always would. She had been trying too hard to set him at a distance so she would not humiliate herself by collapsing into his arms and covering him with frantic kisses until she truly believed he was a fact and not fantasy.

'That lie I was dead has kept you safe.'

'Safe but half alive,' she argued. 'And why would anyone feel they had a right to punish *you* for a traitor's sins, Will? They got him killed when all is said and done; you were only the one who found them out.'

'Whatever their twisted reasoning, my mother was brutally killed. Hearing about it made me realise the friend I reported that treachery to was right, my death was the only way to make sure those threats to wipe out all my loved ones in order to make me suffer as the writer had suffered stopped. My friend did not knew about you, though, or how truly terrified I was for my dearest one of all. You were always the best way to make me sorry I was ever born if that wild beast found out about you and threatened your life. You are my wife, my secret love, and of course I had to die to keep you safe.'

It was my fault then, all that harsh suffering you took on yourself was for me, her inner lover wailed.

And if she wasn't very careful, she would cry again and he would hate it.

'I was alive, but not truly living without you, Will,' she told him shakily. It had hurt her so much to lose him and she was human enough to want him to know it was nowhere near as neat a solution as he stubbornly thought it was five years ago and even now from the stubborn look on his face. 'What if your mother's death really was a crime of passion and that message an ugly threat to make you wary of spying out more traitors while you were counting up troop movements and mapping potential battle sites? What if it was meant to stop you looking too hard at everyone associated with your traitor?'

'How could I stand around arguing with

him when my enemy had said my trials were only beginning and promised the torments of the damned before he was done with me? You were always his best way of taking me straight to hell.'

'Oh, dear, I wonder why?' she said airily, despite the awful knowledge she was the reason he agreed to wipe himself off the face of the earth, taking the threat with him.

'You are my wife; it's obvious.'

'Only if he knew you had one. Nobody has found out about me in six and a half years, so how was your avenger ever going to know about me and try to do you harm by attacking me?'

'I don't know, but how could I take the risk he would find you one day and come after you anyway?'

Chapter Six

Helena saw such bleakness in Will's eyes she supposed she should take this threat seriously as it had cost him so much already. Whoever had made it managed to hit his sore spot by accident, but they could only do it because Will had married her in secret in the first place. She had pushed at his resistance, stoked his desire until it was so hot he succumbed to it despite all his gentlemanly scruples. She had always known he would marry her if he did that, because he was such an honourable man under the dash and dare of the pleasure-seeking young officer on leave.

She was the one who had refused to wait until the war was over to marry him. He was the love of her life and about to risk his all for his country once again so she could hardly wait another day for sweet satisfaction because if she did it might never happen. She had handed someone the perfect weapon to use against him without them even knowing they had it. He had become someone he should never have been for her sake and how sharply that fact stung her now.

'You allowed yourself to be listed among the dead in battle to protect me,' she said flatly and felt a burden of guilt on her own shoulders this time.

'Mostly,' he said, as if admitting it fully might bite him back.

'And you are still doing it. That's why you didn't come to find me when the French left Spain or Napoleon left Elba, or even since Waterloo. It is why I am still the wife nobody but my friend Kate knew you had until today.'

'Besides the vicar who married us and his verger,' he admitted.

'Both of them were so elderly I doubt they are still alive and even if they are why would they tell anyone about us after all these years?'

'I have spent the last five years ferreting out the deepest, darkest secrets of the enemy, so who better than me to know that no secret is ever truly safe?'

'Ah, but you are good at it,' she replied. He would never have been offered such a dark disguise if he wasn't worth the effort of killing off and keeping him that way.

'What has that got to say about anything even if it were true?'

'Your enemy is not that clever, or he would have known hurting your mother might prick your conscience, but it was hardly likely to plunge you into dark despair. Whether he really did it or not, which I doubt, it was a clumsy move at best.'

'He didn't have much to work with, though, did he? Thank God he didn't find out about you and if he truly wanted to hurt me, he could hardly have gone after the men who stood between me and an earldom. If I inherited my uncle's title, I would have been rich and powerful enough to hire a private army to protect me and my family and that doesn't look like a very good revenge to me.'

'I don't see how he could have found out about me when you had sworn me to such secrecy I could not even write to you.'

'It was a chance I could not take, Helena. Now we finally have peace and I have left the Army it is not in their interest to keep quiet about me any more so I had to come here before the scandal broke and mention of my name jogged someone's memory, even in the remote parish where we were wed.'

'Unlikely.'

'But not impossible.'

'No, and I suppose I have to be grateful you think so or I might have gone to my grave not knowing I was still married to you.'

'Don't,' he said with a visible shudder. 'And I would have had to come here anyway. Someone broke into my uncle's safe at Deepdale last week and left the will I lodged with him before Waterloo on the desk in the Estate Office where anyone who went in there could see it.'

'Well, what about it?' she said with a shrug.

'I named you as my sole heir and under your married name so I could be sure it was not challenged,' he admitted, as if he ought to be ashamed of himself. 'When I came home in March this year I learned your father's debts had eaten up your fortune and I could not leave you penniless if I was killed behind the lines trying to find out what Boney was up to this time.'

'As if money would matter when you were about to run such terrible risks again and I didn't even know you were alive to do so.'

'How could I leave you poor when I had the means to set you free?'

'Free? You really think that was freedom? And your uncle knew you were still alive last winter, but you didn't tell *me?*'

'I wanted to be sure you never wanted for anything; I wanted to protect you.'

'*Protect* me? How was hurting me so much anything of the sort, Will?' she demanded. 'I could not mourn you even with my family. I felt so raw and lost when I heard you were dead and you can't understand even a tenth of the pain I feel right now, knowing you were alive all this time and chose not to tell me.'

'It was safer for you not to know,' he said stubbornly.

'What's the point of safety at such cost? You have no idea how bleak my life was when I thought you were dead,' she said and her trust in him as an honourable man who loved her wavered.

What if he wasn't the man she had always thought him? What if he had shrugged her off to embrace a secretive life of outwitting the enemy with sneaky tricks and loved the dare and furtiveness of getting away with it time after time? She eyed him warily. No, she decided; a man who found all that easy would not look as if he had seen into hell since the last time she saw him. His distaste for his secretive life was written on his silver-dusted hair and the stony aloofness he was still trying to hide his true self behind. She acquitted him of discarding her easily, but his shrug and the way he avoided her eyes said he still thought his lies were justified.

'A lie kept you alive,' he said, as if that was all that mattered.

'I told you, I was only half alive. *I* felt dead inside while I tried to mourn my father. He may have left us mired in debt, but he was a kind father and a good husband until the gaming tables stole him away from us. Because of you, his death never felt quite real to me, and I was ashamed that it gave me an excuse to work so hard after he died and Edward could not afford bailiffs or a land steward. That way

I could drive myself so hard I could even sleep for a few hours in a bed that felt so empty because you were never in it.

'So, please, don't talk to me about being safe while you suffered; don't pretend you could not trust me to keep your deepest secrets when I have kept this one for six and a half years,' she said with such impotent fury he must know how he had hurt her now. Yet even without the tears waiting behind her eyes again, their silence felt prickly and he was wearing his I-know-best look. '*And* Waterloo was over two months ago,' she added crossly. 'You were in no hurry to tell me you had survived it as well as everything else, were you?'

'I *am* ashamed of hiding in corners and hurting you with a false report of my death, Helena, but it was still the right thing to do.'

'If you can't see that you have hurt me unbearably maybe we should live apart,' she said with a heavy sigh. 'I had made plans for a new life before you came back from the dead. Maybe I should go through with them and forget I ever had a husband—you seem to have found it easy enough to forget you have a wife.'

'No, I didn't and we married for life. What were you planning to do without me?' he barked as if he thought she really did have a secret lover.

'What does it matter now?'

'It matters to me.'

'I cannot imagine why.'

'Then try harder,' he bit out as if she was intent on torturing him.

'You left me behind all those years ago, but cannot endure the idea of me being happy with someone else,' she accused him recklessly.

'Do you have a lover for me to kill, then?' he said with a hard, possessive glare that said he had been expecting this all along.

'Why would I want one of them when loving you hurt so much?'

'Is that true?'

'That you hurt me or I don't have a lover? Both—and since *I* am not a liar you will just have to believe me.'

'You thought you were free so why wouldn't you be happy?' he said and she preferred fury to the slump of his shoulders and blank look, as if he accepted her right to a lover in his absence when it was unthinkable.

'Because I learned the lesson *you* taught me,' she sniped at him and felt petty. She had learned passion and sensuality and head-long, glorious satisfaction as well as pain and grief from loving him. 'It is impossible for me to love anyone else but you,' she admitted gruffly at last.

'I don't blame you,' he said with a wry grimace and didn't seem to think she meant she still loved him. 'No lover, then, so what *were* you going to do?'

'Help Kate Herridge raise her fatherless children and keep the estate in good order for her eldest boy until he is of age.'

'You two always were more like sisters than friends so I suppose it makes sense,' he said as if it might still work. How could he even think she would make a life apart from him now she did not have to?

'Kate will understand,' she said and crossed her fingers because Kate sounded desperate for help with four young children and a sprawling and un-modernised estate held in trust for a six-year-old baronet.

'I dare say we can both help her if only we can untangle this mess and you would be more exposed to attack in the wilds of Derbyshire without a man of the house to make a villain think twice about attacking you.'

'Perhaps we should both go, then.'

'And endanger her and her children as well? Even I am not that much of a fool.'

'Then we must track your threat down and set you free so we can both help her as she has always helped me. How do you suggest we go about it?'

'*We* won't; *I* shall deal with my enemy while my uncle and his people keep you safe at Deepdale.'

'If you think I will sit about being *protected* for even one more day you need to think again, Will. I would track this enemy of yours down on my own rather than sit around waiting for you to own up to me when you are not so busy.'

'No!'

'I won't wait patiently to find out your fate this time so choose an option, Will.'

'How could I protect you while I am hunting down my enemy?'

'By being extra-resourceful or trusting me

to look after myself. I have done so without you for so long after all.'

'Don't remind me,' he said gruffly.

'I will if it makes you see me as the independent woman of eight and twenty I am rather than the widgeon you appear to think I am.'

'Then I shall have to accept the lesser of two evils and take you with me,' he said crossly.

'Promise?' she replied suspiciously.

'I promise to take you with me when I leave Hawley Park today,' he said but that wasn't good enough for her.

'And you won't sneak off into the night or leave me somewhere to be called for after you have dealt with your enemy?'

'I suppose if I do you will take the second option and go after whoever it turns out to be on your own?'

'Of course I will.'

'Then I promise to keep you with me rather than risk having you running about the countryside getting in the way.'

'Don't think you can divert me by being rude, Will Harborough, and I do know you have not promised me exactly what I asked you to.'

'How did it go, then?'

'I promise not to sneak off in the night or leave my wife somewhere safe until my enemy is caught and dealt with…' She trailed off and waited for him to say the words that would let her know he would not do either of those things. 'And I trust your word even if you don't, Major.'

'Very well, I promise not to do any of that either,' he said so wearily she had to believe him.

'And if you break that oath, I shall haunt you until your real dying day.'

'If you have to haunt me, I hope that's sooner rather than later.'

'Ah, no, Will, let's not talk about either of us dying for another sixty years or so. You can promise me that along with the rest while you're about it.'

'Even I am not so rash as to promise us so much time together, Lady Helena,' he told her and suddenly she really did believe there was a future for them and it made her heart sing despite this avenger on his tail and all the terrible things he must have seen and maybe even done these last five years.

'Promise you will at least try to live and love with me until we're both ninety?'

'That's a very large promise.'

'Just the alive bit then,' she said ruefully.

'No, all of it and only with you,' he said recklessly.

She so desperately wanted to believe him she didn't dare say another word in case she gave away her eagerness to love him again anyway. Apparently, he thought he had said enough as well so they stared at the artful green space around them in silence. If he was anything like her, he wasn't seeing what was in front of him. Senses only half alive after he was reported dead were fully alert again now and every inch of her skin felt on fire for his touch. More than his touch—for all of him, she realised with a jar of sensual shock. Yet she could not throw herself into his arms and declare the past six and a half years null and void, could she?

Probably not, she decided, and counted them again in her head. The first year and a half were bad enough, but the next five of mourning him had felt hopeless—so, no, the lying wretch did not deserve any of their old, wild loving yet.

'So, what happens now?' she broke the silence to ask without turning her head to meet his gaze and give herself away.

'Well, we *are* alone up here,' he said with the remains of the old rakish Will in his deep voice, although he was probably only joking.

Hot desire flared in his dark eyes to remind her of her how good that could be and if only it was that easy they could lose themselves in loving and blot out the pain and loneliness in between. Nothing about this situation was easy, though, and she wasn't sure she was that ready to forgive him yet.

'What of it?' she said coolly.

'This,' he said and kissed her anyway.

He tasted so blissfully familiar her lips trembled, then responded before she could say, *No, not here and certainly not now.* Then she didn't care if the whole world knew Will was home and they were going to be lovers again and out in the open at last this time as well.

'Mmm…' she murmured like a gourmet

tasting a rare treat. 'Lover,' she whispered when he raised his head to gasp in breath.

He plunged his tongue so explicitly into her mouth it was clear he was as hungry for her as she was for him. And, yes, this was so delicious. All her senses sharpened where the dear familiarity of his mouth met hers. The slide of their tongues and lips and the delicious, yearning touch of him added to the taste and scent of the one and only love she had missed so cruelly and for so long. Then the shivers of heat shooting through her, the eager sensual excitement all over her, said they had far more than kisses to long for.

Her eager nipples tightened, desire made her breasts feel fuller and richer as they snuggled into his seeking hands. The most urgent of needs settled at the secret heart of her until she wriggled against his delicious, powerful body on the knife edge of exquisite pleasure, eager for everything they were together, needing him so badly after a long, harsh drought and never mind where they were or who might see them.

Yet he stayed silent while she whispered encouraging murmurs, could not keep back the soft little moans of longing for more as his busy hands explored the changes and continuity of her eager body and he stoked the need already almost mercilessly hot inside her. His mouth and tongue drove to their old, lovely rhythm and it felt so sweet and warm and ruthlessly familiar, but she knew he had a sixth sense ever on the alert for the outside world.

There was the new, harder Will holding them back again from being the Helena and Will who had tumbled headlong into love at first sight. She moaned a soft protest this time at the thought he had no right to be keeping even that aloof. She had a right to everything he once was as her lover after what he had done to them and she grew restless in his arms even as the fire inside her protested. She felt him drawing back, but couldn't regret how they'd fallen on one another out here in the open air, like the starving-for-one-another lovers they ought to be after so long apart.

For a moment Will looked as dazed and shocked by the familiar yet strange alchemy ready to blaze through all the lies and sorrows between them as she was. 'We must go,' he said as he drew even further away with a sigh of regret—well, it had better be regret, she decided militantly.

'Did you have a mistress in your other life, Will? Did she make you forget me in her arms?'

She had to ask, because if he truly had six and a half years of pent-up desire driving him nigh demented, would he be able to draw back now and eye her with cooling heat in his unfathomable dark eyes?

'I could never forget you,' he said with a fleeting look of discomfort.

Was that a sidelong admission he had taken a mistress? If he had made love to another woman while she was mourning him so deeply that the rest of his sex was invisible to her, could she forgive him? Maybe. Pride felt less important than him being alive and never mind if he truly loved her. She might have to forgive him in the end, but it would take a lot of forgiving.

'You forgot me so well it became a habit,' she argued.

'The Will Harborough you married never forgot you.'

'But you are not him any more, are you?'

'No,' he said with a heavy sigh—and, oh, please, let it not be for the reason she dreaded the most.

'I suppose we must learn to live with who you are now, then,' she said as levelly as she could with that spectre of him making hot and glorious love to another woman buzzing like a whole nest of wasps in her head.

'Must we?'

'Yes, unless you want to walk alone for ever.'

'I thought I already had.'

'Not from the sound of things.'

'Until today I thought I would have to; I was so sure you would take one look at me and demand a legal separation.'

'Would you have been glad if I had?' she said warily. The very idea of it felt like only a slightly lesser hell than the one he had put her through these last five years, but if he did truly want one would pride make her grant his wishes? Probably not, not with the blazing hunger of their frantic kiss still cooling on their lips and even the chance they could get back a fraction of what they once had.

'I would have gone through with it for your sake, but are you sure you don't want one?'

She would rather have half his attention and know the rest was on his mistress than no Will at all and if that made her a fool for love so be it. 'No, but I want a proper marriage this time. At first, I was married to you, yet not married, and then I was a widow in secret while you pretended to be dead. Now I want to have a home and children with you, not a chilly legal agreement never to bother you again.'

There—it was said. He and his fancy woman would have to work their lives around hers for a change. He could not marry anyone else while she was alive and she could not endure another man touching her so Will could divorce her. It was stalemate, a sad consequence of loving too hotly and impulsively until his duty came between them.

Chapter Seven

'I used to think the only good part of the whole farce was you being free of me,' Will said at last.

'It's not freedom when you have to live broken-hearted and pretend not to be, Will. You don't seem to understand how hard my life felt without you.'

'I must try harder then.'

'Do; you are not the only one who had to hide your true self and suffer in silence.'

'I told you, I did not suffer.'

'You are free to think so, but I know that you did just by looking at you. It's written in the lines on your face and those grey hairs. Your mistress might have your heat and passion, but I know how much you have been hurt while you were lost to *me*. Don't shake your head at me because I know you feel too much and not too little and please stop trying to pretend none of it hurts, Will. I am so tired of being lied to and it feels like the final straw that could break us.'

'I don't have a mistress!' he burst out so fiercely she supposed he must have left the wretched woman in Spain, or Belgium or wherever he had found her. Her thoughts must have been written on her face because he jumped to his feet to stamp up and down before he turned to face her. 'I did not have, *do* not have, never will have a mistress. Is that plain enough for you, Lady Helena? Would you like to summon a lawyer so he can draw up a sworn statement for me to sign in the hope you might finally believe me?'

It wasn't so much his offended look and harshly bitten-out words that made her believe him as the temper and hurt behind them. Tension seeped out of her so suddenly she was glad she was sitting down. 'Oh, good,' she said inadequately and no wonder he cursed in several languages and went back to his pacing. 'Well, it is good,' she told him crossly. 'I wanted to kill her,' she finally admitted.

He halted and stared down at her with brooding dark eyes until they lit with some of his old devilment and he smiled like a cat with feathers in his sharp white teeth and an empty canary cage nearby. 'I wonder why,' he said smoothly and quirked an eyebrow at her to demand more.

'You know why,' she said shortly and refused to look away and pretend she was tamed and dispassionate about Will Harborough nowadays.

'Later,' he promised her silkily.

'Only if you are very lucky,' she told him with her nose in the air.

'Yet somehow I think I will be,' he murmured, but it made her feel smug when he looked away as if she was nigh irresistible temptation all the same.

And I should think so too, her inner wanton whispered. *After all this time he should be blind, deaf and dangerous with wanting me instead of doing his damnedest to frustrate us both until dark.*

'That's for me to know and you to find out,' his wife told him snootily instead.

'I always did enjoy your hot temper and

haughty looks, my lady,' he said as if he was recalling them very fondly indeed and there was another piece of their shared past with which to chip away at the walls he had built around himself.

'Making up after one of our arguments always was spectacular,' she conceded and he swallowed hard and looked away. 'Remember?' she said huskily.

'Of course I do, but I am not making love to you until there are four good walls around us and half a regiment outside to keep you safe,' he said sternly.

'Spoilsport,' she murmured sulkily.

'Hussy,' he countered.

'Do I repulse you?' she asked because she had to know how he had managed to step back from making love to her if he truly was faithful to her all this time and now she believed he had been; he had sworn it was so it had to be true. 'I am thin and faded and at my last prayers.'

'No, you are not. What you are is slender and magnificent and if you are not sought after by every single gentleman in the county that's probably because you made it clear you didn't want to be. Can't you tell how much I want you, Helena?' he said hoarsely and looked as if he thought she was angling for compliments, but that wasn't it at all.

'Apparently not enough,' she said grumpily.

She could see he was aroused and those breeches should be outlawed in polite company. Knowing he wanted her so urgently only made her frustration burn even deeper. He was yearning for congress with her every bit as hotly as she was for him and he still would not give in and count the world well lost. Apparently, their reunion would be even more of a challenge than she first thought.

'Just be content for now with knowing I find you even more intriguing and argumentative and desirable than when we first met, my lady,' he went on as if he knew she needed convincing after his comment about her thinness and drawing back from making love to her now. 'Adversity has made you better and stronger and how I wish it had done the same for me.'

'It might if you stopped feeling sorry for yourself,' she told him even though his words made her want to cry yet again. That wasn't going to get them anywhere. She hardly knew whether to dance with sheer joy because he was alive or weep for the bleak life he had been living. 'You are sterner and harder to read than my wild young lover, but you are not broken.' He was also complex as a labyrinth, but what was the point loving an ordinary man when she could love him instead?

'I cannot live like a gentleman, Helena,' he argued as if he truly thought he would be impossible as any sort of husband now. 'I sleep in the open when I can and hate living at close quarters with anyone. I once tried to kill a man who was trying to wake me from a nightmare to keep me quiet. Luckily the rogue fought me off and laughed about it every time I set eyes on him and his band of brigands afterwards, but you must see how dangerous I am and avoid me.'

'Nonsense—and I promise not try to wake you when you are dreaming except with a very long stick and from the other side of the room,' she joked and heard him chuckle despite his haunted expression as he thought about what he had nearly done without even trying.

It was such a small thing to be so proud of,

but she heard the echo of her long-lost lover in that deep rumble of amusement and although he soon remembered he didn't laugh much nowadays she refused to stay out of his dark places and tiptoe around him. To do so would mean they never became truly close again and somehow they must learn to live with the good and bad to do that.

Last time they had the delicious secret of their runaway match to bind them, but now they must build an everyday sort of life together because not having one had forced them apart to suffer so long in silence. If they had to build that life with a deranged avenger on their tail, so be it.

'And not even trying to live as husband and wife would make us into cowards this time,' she said, challenging any ideas he still had about slipping away from her for her own protection.

He frowned as if he might have had some and stared into the middle distance as if he was looking for inspiration. 'And we can't have that, can we?' he said at last.

'No, *we* cannot.'

'Then please promise me you will try slowly,

Helena,' he almost begged, as if he thought their marriage was so fragile it might shatter if they didn't handle it carefully. Of course he had his parents' poor example to make him think it might, but he would just have to learn she wasn't going anywhere except with him.

'As long as we are both trying and in public this time,' she said.

'I cannot just stand about waiting for this brute to hurt you to punish me. I don't care if we have to hide out somewhere for ever and a day as long as it keeps you safe.'

'But I do and I told you I can look after myself.'

'Not against the odds I have ranged against me. How would you know which of our visitors to shoot before he shot you, my fierce warrior queen?'

'Instinct,' she told him with a sweet, wifely smile. 'But I can't help wondering why your clever spymaster never managed to track down who was threatening you and stop him,' she added because she was curious about the anonymous, almost invisible man he had trusted with his life for so long and it was a puzzle how a man like that could be outwitted so easily that Will had to pretend to be dead all this time.

'The cur never said or wrote enough to give himself away, just said I would taste hell on earth after he had killed everyone I ever loved,' Will said impatiently.

'And your clever friend could not find out who was so close to a traitor they thought they could take such cruel revenge without any risk to themself?'

'The notes were so short my enemy could be French or Spanish or as British as you and me.'

'Then maybe he is too busy in Spain or France to worry about you now.'

'No, he is here, whatever his nationality.'

'Why are you so sure?'

'Because whoever broke into my uncle's safe recently could have taken everything valuable he could carry away with him, but he chose to leave it all behind and only leave my will out in the open to say he was there. Who but my enemy would go to such trouble for no reward at all? It was his way of telling me my deepest secret is no longer safe. Now he knows I am alive after all and you are my wife and he could strike any moment, probably when we least expect him to because that's how assassins work. Nobody knows that better than I do,' he said grimly.

Her heart hammered erratically at the thought of him doing such dirty work as a spy. If he had killed stealthily, it would have been to protect his comrades and save more lives than he took. He was nothing like the beast he seemed so convinced had crept into his mother's bedchamber and plunged a knife into her heart time after time, but *Nothing personal, Lady Aurelia.* How could killing a defenceless woman at close quarters be anything *but* personal? Another sliver of doubt added to the ones she already had because that tragedy did not look like a coldly planned crime. If someone *had* staged that poor woman's death to make Will take him seriously, then the perpetrator had a dangerous weakness for melodrama. She really had to think much harder about this matter when she wasn't so busy making sure Will would not leave her behind again.

'I will be careful, then,' she promised, 'but

I cannot and I will not pretend we two are not married any longer.'

'Stubborn, impulsive, ungovernable female,' he snapped and jumped to his feet to pace as if it was the only way he could stop himself shaking some sense into her.

She refused to cave in and agree to them spending more time apart. He needed to forget the half-life he had disappeared into five years ago, even if it killed them both, and, if she ever met his former spymaster, she was going to give him the scolding of his life for the ingenious, cruel solution he came up with to hide Will from his enemy. The man had used Lady Aurelia's brutal death to gain a clever and effective spy and she knew Will was both since he was still alive and had been recalled to do it again this spring. Clearly the Duke of Wellington valued his skills and judgement, even if Will did not share his austere commander's opinion of him.

Will stopped pacing to stare at her as if struggling to work out his next move since she was being so stubborn. 'What would you have me do, Helena?' he asked with an impatient shrug but a hint of vulnerability in his dark eyes.

Because of it, Helena fleetingly considered the idea of staying here without him but, even if she could endure the thought on her own account, she could not take such risks with her family. Hawley was a gentleman's residence, not a fortress, and the thought of anyone harming her brother or Mattie and their unborn baby, or the Dowager, simply to hurt Will through her, felt horrifying. It was a valuable insight into how Will must have felt when he was declared dead to protect her, but it was one more reason why she could not stay here.

'I am coming with you,' she said, 'and the sooner the better.'

'I need to plan a safe route, find some men to guard us,' he argued as if the whole idea of her leaving with him was all but impossible.

'I doubt your nemesis will wait for you to gather a private army and we have to lead him away from my family right now.'

'This is too hasty; we need to prepare properly,' he grumbled.

'You are not leaving here without me and don't bother to argue because I will find a way and when I do, I might never let you out of my sight again.'

'Could be awkward,' he said wryly and she smiled at him like an idiot because he sounded so like the old, dear Will.

'Or you could be a very lucky man,' she murmured throatily.

'Later,' he said huskily and looked away again.

'Serves you right for laughing at me,' she said as he cleared his throat and stamped about a bit to distract himself from wanting her visibly all over again.

'If we must go, I had best get you away from here before you decide to put on one of your warrior ancestor's suits of armour and charge into battle on my behalf.'

'I would if I needed to. I would make use of all the power and influence my family and yours can wield against a coward who attacks in the shadows, Will, but I know that would take time and careful planning and you are in a hurry.'

'I thought that was you, my lady, but if we are going, we need to be gone in time to get somewhere safe by nightfall. At this rate we will be standing here arguing about it when the moon rises.'

'Some of us can talk and plan at the same time,' she said haughtily.

'Termagant,' he accused and his grin made her heart race and that familiar twist of need grind again, so she was the one who had to turn her head away in order not to beg for his husbandly attentions this time.

Chapter Eight

At last Pensham hurried up to the folly and Will decided it was probably safe to leave him and Helena to work out how she could leave Hawley without anyone else knowing who she had left with. They were soon busy planning for her to borrow some of her sister-in-law's clothes, since Her Ladyship could not wear most of them while she was big with child. Then she needed to write an urgent message to her best friend, Lady Herridge, which her brother's personal groom would take to Kate to let her know that Helena needed to pretend she was riding to Derbyshire in a grand hurry after an urgent summons from her best friend.

Will left the brother and sister working out details for Helena's hasty departure and strode away to make his own plans for an unexpected journey with his stubborn lady in a very different direction.

To get away without Helena following in his footsteps, he had been forced to solemnly promise he would be back within the half-hour. After adding up those five years of lying he decided he could hardly blame her for not trusting him much further than she could throw him. He got to the copse where his friend was waiting with a restless team and Lord Flamington's dashing racing curricle and hoped Greystone would adapt to this situation as easily as he always had to a crisis when they were in the field together.

'What took so long?' his friend and former spymaster demanded sharply.

He supposed Grey, who was unmarried, had no idea how shocked a wife must be when her supposedly dead husband came back to her from the grave. Will thought he had been remarkably quick under the circumstances and it felt like a snip at Helena for Grey to believe he should have been quicker at shaking her whole world to its foundations. He didn't like feeling distance yawn between him and the man who had stood by him at the darkest time of his life so far, but he also refused to set Helena's shock and the gallant way she had recovered from it at naught.

'We need to make another plan, Grey. I have to ask you for another huge favour,' he replied even as he tried to work out how to do it without help if he had to.

Maybe being with Helena had heightened his perceptions, but Will thought he saw a flash of annoyance in his friend's cool grey eyes before they were as unreadable as glass again.

'What is it? What has gone wrong?' Grey demanded urgently.

Of course Will was mistaken. Grey stood by him when nobody else could and he had dropped everything to help deal with this latest disaster when he received Will's message that his enemy knew he was alive and now had the perfect target to take his revenge on, one even Grey had not known about until Will told him he had a wife.

'Not exactly gone wrong, just different,' he said. 'I must take Lady Helena into hiding with me, Grey. Now I know Pensham's Countess is about to present him with their first child and can see for myself Hawley is far too open and vulnerable to a swift attack, I cannot leave her here now that devil knows I am alive and was married to her all along. Pensham is too preoccupied with his wife to be able to protect my wife around the clock as I can since it has been the very purpose of my useless life for so long.'

'You are too hard on yourself, but I suppose your wife would be safer at Deepdale with your uncle,' Grey said with a sage nod as if that was the best plan.

'Not when that damned rogue has already managed to get so far inside Lord Flamington's domain without a soul being any the wiser,' Will said with a fleeting frown of his own because it felt as if Grey was not taking the danger Helena could be in seriously enough or he would already have realised Deepdale would not do either.

'What are you going to do with her, then?' Grey said.

Had his old friend always been this irritating or had this latest crisis in Will's life wearied Grey of finding neat ways to get him out of trouble? The latter, of course, as Grey found him once in the worst trouble Will had ever faced, without his friend even knowing how terrible it was until now. Will already owed the man Helena's life, then, and he felt very guilty when he realised how little he wanted his friend's company now he had Helena's to look forward to instead.

Ungrateful swine, he accused himself.

'Take her with me, of course.'

'What the devil for?'

'If I need to explain that she is feeling neglected after being deceived into believing I was dead for so long, I advise you never to take a wife, Grey,' he joked, but his friend did not laugh.

'She has been your biggest weakness all these years so why am I not surprised? At least I know now why you were so desperate for the cover I offered when you finally decided to use your Spanish heritage and command of the language to help your country.'

'And why I was so reluctant to do it in the first place.'

'I thought that was because you are a gentleman and they don't take to our grubby profession unless forced to by the direst of circumstances,' Grey said bitterly. 'I did it because I lack a great family to push my promotion and had to get on by using what means came to hand and spying served me well enough.'

'I gained my captaincy on merit,' Will said stiffly.

'I didn't mean *you* bought your promotion. Ignore me, Will, I am too bitter that my nip-farthing great-uncle never lifted a finger for me as a boy beyond pushing me into the Army and washing his hands of me so he didn't have to pay my school fees any longer.'

'He was a hard man, but he did leave you New Court when he turned up his toes this summer.'

'Lucky for me that he sent me away, then, since he fell out with all my cousins and I was the only one not here to be disinherited.'

'And now you have a grand old house and estate as well as Wellington's less than effusive gratitude for a job well done.'

'True and never mind about me—what do you intend to do with your wife?'

'Take her to New Court for tonight, if you'll allow me to? You have half the rogues under your former command working on it so at least she should be safe there for the night.'

'Keep your friends close and former comrades even closer,' Grey said flippantly. 'The three of us will have a cramped journey and I'm not sitting up behind.'

'No, I hope you will ride to Derbyshire instead of playing bodkin between me and my lovely wife for the rest of the day.'

'Why the devil should I?'

'Because you are the only person I trust to go to Herridge Hall and make sure Lady Herridge is also safe from my enemy. They are closer than most sisters and Lady Helena was due to go there and help Her Ladyship now she is a widow. My wife won't even consider the idea now I am home, before you suggest she go north instead.'

'Of course she must not, she would be much too vulnerable and of course I will do as you ask. After all we have been through, how could I refuse?' Grey's generous offer made Will ashamed of his fleeting doubts that his one true friend was not as true as he had always thought him.

'What a magnificent team of horses,' Helena said when Will pulled up his uncle's very dashing curricle and team a few miles from Hawley so she could scramble into the high seat. She was glad of all those days in the saddle twice over as they seemed to have left her limber enough to manage it alone. Will could hardly jump down and help when his horses would probably gallop away without either of them free to keep them in line.

She settled herself and he just tickled his leaders with the long whip and caught it again with such skill she tried not to gape at him. They were soon racing along when the roads were good enough to allow it and she frowned at not having met Will's mysterious friend— the one who accompanied him to Edward's house—so she could judge his motives and character for herself.

She had handed the horse she rode away from Hawley to Edward's head groom so he could leave it at the agreed place for the mysterious Mr Greystone to retrieve and ride wherever he had agreed with Will he should go. Back to Deepdale in order to protect it and Will's uncle from more invaders, she supposed with a preoccupied frown. Maybe secretive men like him always made sure nobody could swear they were anywhere at any given time, but the furtiveness of that handover made her uneasy. This stranger knew so much about her and hers and she knew nothing in return, but she supposed Will trusted the man so she should try harder to do the same.

'And a magnificent driver,' she added as Will held the spirited team to a sedate trot behind a dray until the road ahead was clear and they could have their heads again. 'When did you find the time to learn to drive to an inch?'

'My uncle insisted we all practised until we stopped being cow-handed,' Will said distractedly.

She supposed she should let him drive and stop trying to distract herself from the mature strength of his vigorous body next to hers. It was so long since she was driven in such a fashionable vehicle, she had forgotten how intimate it felt to sit so close to the driver on the narrow seat. Wondering about Will's peculiar upbringing might stop her yearning for him quite so ardently during the hours she suspected they must get through before he was ready to stop for the night, though, and she had to find some way to distract herself from him if she was not to betray herself as a very needy woman indeed.

'My uncle insisted on lending me his nattiest equipage to get to a safe place as fast as possible, but I'm not sure it was such a good idea when it is so distinctive.'

'We might as well travel in style while we can,' she said with a shrug and wondered where they were going.

Somewhere safe and well protected, she decided, and tried to calculate how far these perfectly matched bays could go. If there was ever a team of sixteen-mile-an-hour carriage horses, this was it, but though darkness would not fall for another six or seven hours at this time of the year, even a fine team like this would slow if kept in harness too long and a change of horses was sure to slow their progress as well. Sixty miles was probably as far as they could possibly get today and even that seemed unlikely.

They would be a long way from Hawley by dusk if Will could endure the strain of handling a spirited team that long. They might get almost into Wales or right through the Midlands and heading north by sunset. At least she had a pretty good sense of direction and knew they were not heading for Lord Flamington's famously grand Deepdale House. She wished Will would trust her enough to tell her where they were bound. Fair enough for him to watch every word he said when he was an intelligence officer and one unwary one could cost him his life, but he was a civilian now and she *was* his wife.

'You intend to draw your enemy away from our families, don't you?' she said after they passed through a toll gate and Will had this ticket and probably every other one between here and wherever they were going ready.

He had intended to make this journey with his friend and not his wife, but she must not be jealous of his close connection to his elusive friend, not with Will alive at her side when only this morning she woke up thinking he was dead. She tried to accept the wonder of him wonderfully, powerfully alive, but she couldn't simply sit here and thank her lucky stars as the world shot past mile after mile.

'Maybe,' he said, eyes fixed between his lead horse's ears as if saying even that much and with nobody listening was almost too much of a risk.

'I presume the speed of this fine team is meant to prevent an attacker getting a good shot at us?'

'Yes,' he said with a quick, hard look to say he didn't even want to think about it with her beside him.

'Then don't treat me like an idiot.'

'Perish the thought,' he muttered gloomily and she had to smile because they sounded like a long-married couple bickering and that felt ridiculously precious for some odd reason.

'Before you start feeling guilty about not being able to endure a closed carriage for my sake, know that I prefer to travel like this. If we are chased, I prefer to know it and I only ever liked them when you were in a better mood.'

'Don't remind me,' he grumbled again, as if their delicious morning ride through the Derbyshire countryside after they were married was haunting both of them now.

'Later,' she promised him with a smug echo of his earlier promise to make him realise how frustrating it was.

'Witch.'

'Happy to hear that you still think so, Husband.'

'That's one of us, then.'

After that half-serious exchange they were both silent for several miles. Helena tried to distract herself with nature just as Will had done on their wedding morning and for very similar reasons. She needed to divert herself from the delicious friction of his body next to hers, mile after tortuous mile. The unique scent of him made her supposed fascination with ripening corn and orchards heavy with fruit a myth. Apart from dust and sun-warmed fields and woods she could smell warm man, fastidiously clean before he set out and with just a hint of lemon water left over from his morning shave.

The rest of it was him. The scent of Will— her man—and it made her want to groan out loud with frustration. She needed to explore the changes and constants of her only ever lover, but they were in the middle of what was probably Worcestershire countryside by now. Wouldn't that be a surprise, for any wandering bumpkin if they found Lord Flamington's finest team of outrageously expensive horses unattended.

The sultry warmth of the day made her inner madwoman speculate about the feel of summer-heated air on her bare skin as she and Will made love without anything between them in the nearest field. Impossible, of course—it was a scandalous idea, even if they had had a disapproving groom or tiger to hold the bays while they were busy being very married indeed. It was beyond even the effrontery of the daring lover she became the day she met Captain Will Harborough and certainly beyond his sternly mature successor.

Major Harborough was so fearful for his wife's safety she could feel the tension in his sleekly muscular body and it was probably vain to hope even their old, fierce passion could distract him from that until they were safely indoors with a stout door between them and the world.

And you say that dull and dutiful Lady Helena Snowe was caught cavorting nude and in broad daylight with a mystery lover? How deliciously shocking, my dear, and perhaps she is not quite as dull and worn out as we all thought her when she retired to the country to do whatever it is they do there.

Helena imagined the gossips saying such things about her and didn't care. Being outside polite society for so long must have cured her of even the slightest inclination to please the tabbies instead of herself and Will. However, if she didn't find a way to distract herself from the scandalous idea of them resuming the intimacies of lovers sooner rather than later, she would drive herself distracted, so, she went back to brooding on the reason for all this driven haste instead.

'We could just announce to the world that your gravestone lied, Will, and tell it we have been married all this time as well. Then we could wait for your enemy to come to us. At least we would be ready to deal with him on our own terms that way,' she suggested and felt him flinch at the very idea.

He believed he had a devious and dangerous enemy on his tail and she should learn to tread more gently on his sensitive spots. This one had cost him so much; the price was written in his wary expression and once raven-dark hair so she must learn to consider his feelings again as well as expect him to do the same for her. They had never had the chance to learn to be erring and striving people together, as well as lovers, last time. They had had no time for such a luxury when they were young and he clearly didn't think they had enough for it now, but he had to be wrong.

'Don't you even think seriously about announcing it to the world until I deal with this snake,' he said with such a fierce frown at the plodding cart in their way the driver stared at him with wide-eyed shock as they swept past in a cloud of dust and arrogance.

'Why not, Will? It's high time we admitted who we really are and dared the devil,' she insisted once they were clear.

'What sort of monster do you think I am, Helena? I would never take such a criminal risk with your safety simply to flush out a vindictive killer. I really would want to die this time if he managed to get to you after I had set you up as a mark for him to shoot at. And no,' he said when she opened her mouth to argue, 'please don't even try to persuade me black is white on this occasion.'

'Major Harborough commands and his meek

little wife blindly obeys him, even when she knows he is wrong?' she said with such heat he forgot to be terrified for her and gave her a rueful grin before focusing on his team again.

'Would that be the same wife who never knowingly obeyed a *request* of mine without arguing that same bit of black was white before she did so?'

'The very same and why not, Will?'

'Because it could get you killed,' he said flatly, 'and as I never had a gravestone how could it tell lies about me?' he added to let her know that part of their conversation was closed.

'Yes, you did, or rather I paid for one and I hope the people who claimed they were going to provide it did not swindle me. I suppose I had better arrange for it to be taken down and broken up now you are alive again, now I think about it, though.'

'Not yet, but you really paid for a memorial stone for me?' he said and at first seemed shocked she'd bothered, then frowned again as the full implications must have occurred to him. 'Any fool could have found out who paid for it to be carved and put up and come after you,' he said as if her grief-stricken gesture could have carelessly given their secret away before it had properly begun.

'I did it anonymously and before my father died, lest you're wondering where I found the money. That's one small part of my family's wealth I managed to waste instead of him. So at least he didn't manage to toss that bit away on the turn of a card, even if it does turn out to have been wasted on your lying gravestone,' she told him impatiently.

'Who did you get to act for you, then? It obviously wasn't your brother, unless he's the finest actor never to grace the London stage since I am sure he had no idea you were married to me until I told him so just now,' he said as if this was a whole new level of worry to add to an already fine crop of them.

'Your uncle,' she said bluntly and saw shock and a hint of betrayal in his eyes before he forced himself to concentrate on the horses again. She should not have started such a fraught conversation while he was driving a spirited team, but how else could she get him to face the things she knew he would walk away from if he was free to do so? This was a discussion they needed to have so it might as well be sooner rather than later.

'The Earl?' he said and she nodded. 'So he has known about us all this time and said nothing about it even after the burglary and that damned will was left lying about for anyone to read?' he added as if he could hardly believe his ears.

'Yes, I went to Deepdale about a fortnight after you were listed dead and I was heavily veiled before you get in a fine tizzy about me going there at all. He most certainly knew I was your secret widow and promised to do what I wanted and not tell anyone I was the one who wanted it in your local churchyard. As far as I know, he did what I asked and has kept my secret safe ever since.'

'Even from me,' Will said tightly and as if he hated the idea of the two people he was closest to in the world keeping such a secret even from him. 'Uncle Peter never said a word about you, not even when I reappeared at Deepdale so furtively before the Waterloo Campaign and demanded his silence about that as well.'

'Ah, but you already knew you were married to me so why would he tell you about it?' she said sarcastically, but he seemed too pre-occupied to even notice.

'He never even gave me a hint that he knows I am married to you, the cunning old devil—the very opposite, in fact.'

'Perhaps he is too subtle to be so clumsy.'

'The old fox.'

'There's no need to sound so put out about it, Will. He promised not to betray me to a living soul and he was only keeping his word.'

'A little too well, but why did he threaten to push every unwed female in the area in my direction when he already knew I was married to you?'

'*Because* he knew you were already married to me, I imagine,' she said with a regal look and a challenge. She admired the Earl's style even if his nephew looked as if he would like to strangle his only remaining Harborough relative.

They were forced to stop talking when they reached the outskirts of Worcester and Helena felt the pent-up tension in Will's sleekly powerful body throughout the stop-and-start journey across that ancient city. She cursed whoever was behind this creeping threat he was so afraid would reach out to destroy her even in the midst of this hubbub.

At last they were through the tangles and bustle and obstacles and he was driving across the New Bridge over the River Severn and they were heading west. She vaguely recalled someone once saying there was a pinch of Welsh blood in the Harboroughs, so perhaps he had distant family in that mysterious, almost magical land. She had always wanted to know more about the Principality, but being so absorbed in Edward's ailing estates meant she was bound to them when their father died in debt. Maybe she would have the chance to explore Wales and find out what was legend and what was fact in Will's company and her eyes went dreamy at the very thought of a protracted and very belated journey through the most romantically rugged parts of it.

Chapter Nine

'Are you too tired to go on?' Will asked her when they stopped to change horses a couple of hours later.

'Didn't you hear me say I have helped my brother manage his estates for the last four and a half years? All I have done today is sit here admiring the scenery while you did all the work, so why would *I* be the weary one?'

'Then you don't mind if we carry on?'

'I would be insulted if we didn't because you think I am some sort of die-away miss, or maybe we should make that a missus.'

'Neither title fits you; you have always been a fine lady.'

'So I might be, but I am still your wife and not such a feeble one either.'

'You are happy to go on, then?'

'Of course,' she said firmly. As the ostlers rushed to hold the horses' heads her husband jumped down from his high seat and helped her down as she was still his wife and a lady and he refused to leave her to scramble down from her perch by herself this time.

She got down with as much dignity as she could and went inside to be fussed over by the landlady of the coaching inn. Apparently even wearing a shabby gown and close bonnet to travel in she did not look like a poor man's wife since her husband drove a fine rig like the one they had just rolled up in.

It felt oddly satisfying to be able to openly wear her wedding ring at long last and especially to have such a distinguished husband to be smug about owning up to. She had not been able to wear it on her wedding finger openly and in daylight since the first week of their marriage and it felt so fine and liberating to see the glimmer of fine gold on her left hand again at long last.

Helena had been forced to hide it in her writing case and pretend she was still as single as a nun; she could only wear it briefly when she was alone at night while the Snowes were still rich enough for her to have a ladies' maid. She used to take it off again and hide it before her maid caught sight of it in the morning, but at least poverty had meant Helena could keep it on a chain around her neck all the time as soon as her maid was busy fussing over some other fashionable lady. Then Lady Helena Snowe could dress plainly and simply, as befitted a busy lady of very little means, and lately she had refused to be fussed over and primped for her mother to display her almost-on-the-shelf daughter with style.

Now she left the inn feeling refreshed and very happy to be openly wed to whoever Will was willing to tell the world he was this time. At least being Lady Helena instead of plain Miss Snowe meant not having to lie about that part of being married, but she still walked taller because Will was ready to admit he had a wife at long last, even if she could not tell the polite world she was really Lady Helena Harborough and had been so for years behind their back.

'Better?' he asked her once an ostler had handed her up into the high, light carriage and Will held this new team back while she settled herself next to him.

'Yes,' she said and resisted the urge to fiddle with her ring under the light gloves she had donned again to keep the worst of the dust at bay.

'Have you lost your wedding ring?' she asked him as soon as they were back on the road and heading west again.

'No, it was left on my uncle's desk with my will after that so-called robbery just to reinforce the fact you were not a secret any more. If it makes you feel any better, I will put it on as soon as we stop for the night.'

'Maybe you should think how it would make *you* feel to own up to me as your wife and not worry so much about my feelings about it,' she said stiffly.

'With your ring back on my finger I could almost be at evens with the world again,' he admitted, then seemed determined to concentrate on his horses.

'Almost?'

'Not all the way there until this madman is dealt with.'

'Maybe not even then,' she said distantly

and thought hard about his madman and what a caring wife should do about him.

At least she had the time to think harder about this stealthy avenger of his as the miles flashed by. The more she thought about it, the more unlikely he began to seem. Will was probably still too close to the horror of killing and bloody vengeance the Spanish guerrillas inflicted and endured during a desperate struggle for freedom. He had seen far too much of the massacre of families and rivals, French and Spanish, so of course he took a threat to his loved ones seriously.

She shuddered for his deep-down terror for her all these years and knew he did what he had thought he must to protect her from the same bloody end his mother had suffered. Yet surely that end was the result of Lady Aurelia's recklessly taking lover after lover when age began to take its toll on her almost legendary beauty?

The lady had been trying to reassure herself she was still the same Incomparable as ever by demanding the worship of as many males as she could fit into her chaotic life and never mind if they became jealous of one another or the discarded ones were frustrated by her caprices to the very edge of madness.

Helena had almost been amused by the woman's incessant demands for abject masculine worship at her daintily shod feet and her open contempt for her own sex until she met Will. After that she loathed the woman for abandoning him as a baby. At least Will had been able to grow into a fine man without any help from Lady Aurelia or his soldier father, but this wasn't the time to distract herself from the matter in hand by wondering how he did it.

Logically, it seemed far more likely to Helena that one of Lady Aurelia's lovers was driven mad by her whims than Will's enemy going to such lengths to kill her in order to torture a son the woman rejected as a tiny baby. Whether the man who made those threats was a cold avenger or a wily opportunist, his luck was certainly in on the day that Lady Aurelia Harborough's ran out.

Helena frowned at the gold and green countryside they were driving through at such a clip and tried to imagine herself in war-torn

Spain in the year 1810 alongside Will. There had been one or two victories and some appalling reversals of fortune for Britain and her allies by then and there were some loud demands in both Houses of Parliament for the Army to come home and leave any more fighting to the triumphant British Navy.

Being fluent in Spanish and an exploring officer acute enough to smoke out a traitor must have made Will perfectly fitted to work secretly behind the scenes to gain some advantages that might convince his own side it was still a struggle worth the price of more lives and a great deal more money.

All his would-be masters needed in their struggle to gain those advantages was Will's co-operation and they would not have had that before he thought she was in acute danger. News his mother had been savagely murdered must have been like manna from heaven for his devious masters as he then almost begged them to kill him off to keep the rest of his family safe—and they didn't even know he had a wife to make him so desperate for his enemy to stop his sinister campaign of vengeance.

She had been the weapon even his own side didn't know they had; she was the reason why Will had to spend five years at odds with himself. It stirred up such a tangle of emotions she had to bite back a gasp at the sting of it. If only they had not been wed in secret, if only she had refused to make that promise not to tell the world they were married unless she was with child, he would not have been such an easy target for someone's hatred, or for his masters to manipulate into doing what they wanted if that hatred did happen to be an invention of someone's imagination.

The grand passion she had believed in so fervently and for so long, even when all hope seemed dead, had been the cause of her husband's ills. She felt the agony of knowing it, even if she could not bring herself to regret their marriage because she still loved him so dearly. It was all she could do not to curl up into a ball and wail over the many hurts lurking in his past even so. Five years of concealing her deepest, darkest sorrows came to her aid and made it possible to hold still and stare at the passing countryside instead, but it was a close-run thing.

'Are you all right?' he asked as if he knew she was not somehow. He probably thought she was exhausted after sitting here swaying to the movement of his uncle's beautifully sprung sporting vehicle as it rattled along at a fine pace.

'What a poor honey you do think me, Will,' she managed to say lightly and even smiled at him as if she only had that to worry about.

'You are a woman in a million,' he said bracingly and she shook her head and smiled again, but did not try to disillusion him.

Mile after mile flashed past and occasionally Will would slow the pace for a farm cart or a gig or the lumbering local stage, but most of the time they were lucky and the road was clear.

The harvest was not quite ripe just this little bit further north and west than Hawley, so there were no laden wagons plodding from fields to rick yards and no carts full of apples heading for the cider presses as they would do in a month or so. Even the rich red Herefordshire acres became less rich and more undulating as they drove on into the west, towards the sinking sun.

Helena marvelled at Will's stubborn endurance when he tilted his hat to keep the setting sun out of his eyes. She began to wonder if he would have the strength left for afterwards, for what they had promised one another when they finally reached their destination, wherever that might be. She would have to wait if he had not, she supposed with a huff of frustration. After all she had already done it for so long, she ought to be very good at waiting by now. Yet as they drove relentlessly onwards it seemed as if they might never get to his chosen destination for the night and the feel and fact of him next to her was almost too much for her self-control.

She still wanted to pinch herself every now and again to reassure herself this was not all an extraordinary dream. She had been bereft and locked up in such frozen silence about him for so long, now he was here she felt as if she would not truly believe it until they had made love. Then she would know he was absolutely real beyond all doubt. When he was present in every way she had once dreamed. Only this time, she would not have to wake up with tears soaking her pillow as the grim reality of losing him for ever broke back in.

* * *

'How much further?' she asked as the sun began to sink below the Welsh mountains and she could practically feel the strain it was costing him to keep going as if such a journey was nothing out of the ordinary.

'Impatient for your dinner?' he asked lightly.

'Aren't you?'

'Not exactly,' he said with a wry grimace and it was the first hint he had let slip that he was as conscious of her slender-limbed body next to his as she was of his sleekly powerful one, so he really must be tired.

To distract her from his body so close and provoking such prickly but at the same time outrageously hungry sensations in hers, she went back to thinking about his pretend death. Suddenly, it occurred to her if she was right about his mother and she was murdered by an outraged lover, it was indeed possible there was no vengeful assassin on Will's tail at all. Her instincts were not honed and on continual alert for any sign of trouble as Will's must be, but she had not felt a single prickle of warning since he told her there was a dangerous avenger intent on killing everyone he had ever loved.

She still had no sense they should be running as fast as they could go to get safely away from a silent killer. All she felt was this deep and almost desperate frustration that Will was alive and real and beside her and they could not prove it to one another to their infinite satisfaction time after time until they both truly believed it. Maybe she was too eager to believe in such clever evil because if it was a lie, they would be safe? Or was she simply too eager for that glorious proof they were both alive after all to see anything straight and true right now?

Whatever it was, she sat by his side in the golden half-light of a late summer evening and worked her way through a series of impossible scenarios. At least it made a fine distraction from missing her husband's husbandly attentions when his body was flexing at her side and reminding her with every brush of her skirts against his buckskins how very present he felt.

Getting what you wanted wasn't as satisfying as it was meant to be, Will decided. He had wanted Helena so close to him that nobody could even try to attack her without him knowing about it, but nothing but complete intimacy with her would feel close enough for his wayward body now. He fought a groan at the very thought of how it would feel if they were truly that close again, after the endless years he had spent without her. Merely satisfied, physically sated and that was all, he informed his argumentative, disobedient body sternly as it tried to rebel yet again.

As if she was an appetite you needed answered or an itch to be scratched, it informed him scornfully, and kept on longing for what it wanted so badly that neither his honed willpower nor weariness could overtop it.

He had to stay alert and watchful every inch of the way and now he was so tired he should be immune to her unique allure and want sleep far more than he wanted his wife. Yet it was still impossible to stay alert enough for any danger threatening her with his body so stubbornly intent on enjoying the glorious conflagration of the senses he could only find with her.

And he didn't trust it to stop at only once. He knew need would consume him; every sense and ounce of caution in him would go up in smoke once he let himself off the leash with her again at long last. It felt as if he had been starving and thirsting in a desert for vast spans of time without her.

He had done his best to lock himself away and pretend he was made of marble, but he couldn't do it now that she was so physically close he could feel every slight movement of her supple body as she responded to the quirks in the road and the speed of their travelling.

They had to get to Grey's recently inherited house as swiftly and cleanly as they could, but all he could think about was longing for a locked room in a safe house where they could lose themselves in one another's arms for as long as it took to wear out six and a half years of longing and frustration. A month or so might make a dent in it, but they didn't have the time or peace for such a luxury. Since silence was not stopping his starving, desperate cock longing for her, threatening to be rigidly rampant at any moment and give him away, maybe a little polite conversation would bore it into submission.

What could they discuss to make this gnawing need die down even for a moment? The weather, perhaps, or what she thought about the departure of HMS *Northumberland* with the former Emperor Napoleon aboard and the rumours that it was on its way to a much more secure captivity on the remote island of St Helena? That might do for a while to distract them both from his parlous state, since Helena had always been sharply aware of what went on in the world around them.

Indeed, it got them through several miles and they agreed it looked a harsh exile, but understandable after the emperor's brief one on Elba proved so disastrous for the peace of Europe and cost thousands of lives. They thought about those costly battles to put the great general in exile once again and well out of harm's way and speculated about the new order of Europe without the man who had dominated it for over a decade.

Silence fell again and he wondered how exhausted Helena really was by the constant effort of having to sway with the twists and turns in the road, mile after mile. At this time of year there was still half an hour of setting sunlight for him to drive on through as fast as he dared. Even then he would only just get them to New Court and Grey's unexpected inheritance before darkness fell and they could go no further without it being a terrible risk to them and the horses.

'Would you want to spend most of your time at Deepdale now you are home at last, if an assassin was not threatening me, Will?' Helena asked, as if she knew how tired he was and thought she must keep a conversation going lest he nod off. As if he could with this feral consciousness of her slender feminine curves so intimately close to him. He was nigh on mad with wanting her and not having her for so many miles.

She had seemed so coolly self-contained sitting so close to him all this time. He had no idea if she had noticed how racked with need his stupid body was after enduring the forced intimacy of this narrow bench seat for so long. He was aware of her every move, of the scent of warm woman, and of the unique sound of her voice that he didn't know how much he had yearned to hear again until she spoke to him that first time and it brought back so many memories of it—soft and husky with sated passion and so distinctly hers he had to fight for words to reply.

Goodness knew what he had said to her while he stared at her like a loon across her brother's sitting room only hours ago. But what had she just asked him? He had to concentrate on her words rather than the seductive memories of her voice husky with loving during their all too brief honeymoon. Ah, yes, she wanted to know how he felt about his uncle's sprawling acreage and the grand Elizabethan mansion at the centre of it.

Who cares where we live as long as we spend a couple of months in my lady's bedchamber doing our best to sate my endless need of you, Lady Helena? the brute inside him silently demanded.

His slightly saner day-to-day self decided that a week or two might make a good enough start on that to let her out for fresh air and limited exercise now and again. She would not need much after all the bed sports he had in mind if that fantasy ever came true, but it seemed highly unlikely after what he had done to her these last five years that she would agree to such sensual captivity for the sake of his sanity.

'Not all the time,' he said at last. 'I have a home on the other side of the Welsh border where we could farm and walk whenever the fancy took us and maybe raise a brood of brats away from all the pomp and ceremony of a grand mansion like Deepdale,' he said, though that idea was hardly likely to dampen his urgent desire to start on those brats straight away. What had possessed him to come up with the half-formed idea his Welsh great-grandmother's beloved home could be the perfect place for them to live that idyllic life, if only she could be persuaded to love it too?

'I might not be able to have them, Will,' she said. 'I didn't conceive during our honeymoon and we put plenty of effort into getting me with child during that to make me doubt if I can.'

He heard an echo of the desolation she must have felt when it was clear there would be no child or any announcement Captain Harborough and Lady Helena Snowe had married one another before he left just in case there was one. It was never only because they might have made that child that first night, or at least it was not the only reason they were wed, he wanted to argue. He had been so eager to marry her and never mind their maybe child because he wanted to claim her in every way he could think of so no other man could usurp him in her bed while he was away. Did that make him possibly the most selfish bastard in Christendom?

Yes, guilty as charged, m'lord. Serve me right if she had taken a lover when she thought I was dead and there was no just cause or impediment to her marrying the brute if she wanted to.

'Even a week of frantic lovemaking was hardly long enough to guarantee a pregnancy, my dear,' he said pompously instead of telling her any of that. Perhaps he was even wearier than he thought because now all he really wanted to do was take her in his arms and distract her from all the gaps he had left in her life.

Perhaps if he was a different man, he would have left her free to find a better man than he was and never mind if she was no longer a virgin thanks to lust driven Will Harborough.

If the man truly loved her, Will was sure he would forgive her one impulsive lapse to make sure he had a breathtaking woman like her in his bed for the rest of his life.

'And it doesn't matter to me if we have a pack of brats or one or none at all,' he added because it didn't sound enough reassurance when he had so much stupid jealousy of a man she never cuckolded him with souring his brain. 'There are plenty of unwanted babies and children in need of someone to care for them so it hardly matters if we cannot have any of our own.'

'Like you were, you mean?' she said and wasn't it just like her, to go straight to the heart of the matter and never mind politely shilly-shallying around the edges. 'Unwanted, I mean,' she added in case he had misunderstood her, as if she felt everything had to be spelt out between them after he'd left so many gaps between them last time. It must have felt as if she had hardly known him when he was supposed to be dead and gone, and now she had this battered and aloof stranger to try to get accustomed to instead of her youthful lover.

'Not exactly,' he argued. 'If I was young enough to remember it, I would feel nigh on overwhelmed by the number of people who lined up to take care of me, at least on my father's side, when he went back to his military career with hardly a backward look at his baby son. Uncle Peter was always there for me and I had an older and wiser cousin as well. Then there were my Uncle John, my Spanish grandmother and my Welsh great-grandmother vying to spoil me, so please don't imagine I was a neglected waif, Helena, since the very opposite was true,' he said with a reminiscent smile, thinking of all the reasons he had to be thankful his family had descended with offers of love and a home when his parents failed him and walked away.

Chapter Ten

Whether he was loved by the rest of his family as a boy or not, Helena still felt for a tiny baby who was abandoned by his careless parents, but she knew he would not thank her for her pity, or her anger on his behalf against the selfish couple. 'Is it a Harborough failing to put others first, then?' she said, his five years of silent servitude proving what a gallant idiot he was to do what he did mainly for her. 'With the notable exception of your father, of course.'

'Yes, let's leave him out of things whenever we can, but I suppose it is true of all the others,' he said as if he didn't include himself either and he was the worst offender of all.

She recalled how his heart was wrung by tragedies great and small on the retreat to

Corunna and afterwards and silently argued with him. He might have been loved as a boy, but rejection by both his parents had made its mark on him even before war set its grim stamp on him. And if a scheming rogue had manufactured a threat to his family to make him do what he wanted she would never forgive him even if Will did.

'Ah, here we are at long last. The master of the house is away from home, but we will be safe here,' he said as he turned his weary team off the country road and into a tree-lined lane and the rosy gold light of sunset was lost in shadows. He drove between overgrown hedges along a surprisingly well-kept drive. 'Sanctuary, for tonight, at any rate,' Will added.

Will had told her only two men were trusted with his secrets—well, two more knew them now, but Lord Flamington and Edward were truly trustworthy. Since the Duke of Wellington clearly did not live quietly in the Welsh Marches that left only one man on Will's list of trusted friends who could be the owner of this estate, but right now, she was far more interested in her husband than she was in him.

'There are enough old soldiers here to keep watch while you sleep,' Will said, as if that was all that mattered.

'You don't need any, I suppose? I don't need cosseting so please don't hold back for my sake. I can ride all night if you are game.'

'Maybe you can, but I wouldn't let you, Helena. The night is too full of shadows and potential for an ambush for us to risk going on in the dark.'

'Let me?' she said scornfully. She batted him out of the way when a groom came running to hold the horses' heads and scrambled out of her seat before Will could jump down and hand her down like a fine society lady. '*Let* me, Will Harborough?' she said again, feeling overwhelmed by his misplaced gallantry and stubborn trust in a man she was becoming more and more suspicious did not deserve it.

'You have no right to stop me doing whatever I choose to do after what you have done to me,' she informed him and maybe she needed to be angry so she didn't begin to act like a meek little wife after such an eventful day.

'I have to and you are the most exasperating female I ever met,' he informed her as she stormed off towards the open front door and swept past a butler who looked more like a prize-fighter, hardly even pausing to let Will catch up.

After some colourful curses and saying he never thought for one moment the guest they were ordered to prepare for would turn out to be a ghost, the supposed butler told Will, 'Himself is away.'

'I know,' Will said tersely and hardly even seemed to notice the man's shock at his continued existence because he was so busy glowering at her.

'Do you have a bedchamber prepared for us even so?' she demanded and the man's eyes widened with shock Will had a wife as well as a life. She supposed the servants must be discreet, given their master's profession, so Will probably could trust them not to spread the story he was alive until after he dealt with his devils, real and imaginary.

'Yes, ma'am,' the man said, halfway to a salute before he recalled he was no longer in the Army and she wouldn't be one of his officers even if he was.

'Kindly tell me where it is, then, and don't send our luggage up until we ring for it,' she ordered as if she was a haughty earl's daughter to the very bone. She was almost ashamed of herself, but now temper had got the better of her she managed not to be. '*You* are coming with me,' she informed Will with a regal look and an airy gesture towards the shadowy and ancient-looking staircase.

'Second door on the right at the top of the stairs, missus,' the now grinning manservant called after them.

'I need to discuss extra precautions for tonight with Troughton and make sure he sets lookouts for any strangers lurking in the area,' Will protested.

'Do you trust these men to know what they are doing in peace or war?' she turned around on the stairs and demanded. The unlikely butler and three more old soldiers looking uncomfortable in the everyday livery of footmen were standing at the bottom of them, staring up at the intriguing spectacle of Captain Harborough returned from the dead and with a very haughty wife to make him even more interesting.

'I would never have brought you here if I did not,' Will said as if she was the blind idiot out of the two of them and she profoundly disagreed with him.

'Then stop arguing and do as *I* bid for once in your life, Major.'

'I can't see what the hurry is,' he mumbled grumpily behind her.

'I heard that and you, sir, are an idiot,' she told him and didn't even look at him because she was too busy running upstairs to spare time.

'Now that's plain insulting,' he complained and took the stairs two at a time to catch up and presumably argue some more.

'No, *this* is plain insulting,' she informed him furiously once he stood at the top of the stairs facing her. '*This* stupid pretence that we two are nothing much more than chance travelling companions is an insult. I refuse to be written off as a wife you married in a moment of folly six and a half years ago, William Harborough. I will *not* be a pathetic little mouse-like spouse, eager to accept the fact you are alive and back from the wars and stubbornly determined to protect me like a dog with a bone. A bone you no longer really want, by the way, but think someone else might snatch off you if you don't guard it like the Crown Jewels.'

'It's not like that…' he said, but she could not let him have his say in case she wound down altogether and burst into humiliating tears again. She had never been a watering pot until she met him again and that was yet another reason to be furious with the great, blundering oaf of a *man*.

'It is like that and I've had enough of it. Either you come inside this nice dark bedchamber with me right now or you can go and sleep in the stables with your friends and former comrades, Husband. I want a proper one of those in my bed for the first time in all the weary years since you let me think you were dead and we would never be able to make love to one another again.

'I am so tired of pretending we are no more than two blocks of wood, but if you want to carry on doing so, go away and let me sleep alone because I cannot share a room with you and pretend we are nothing to one another. I am done with pretending about our marriage and I refuse to walk another step that way.'

'Sounds like an offer a man'd be a fool to refuse, *Major*,' the pretend butler shouted upstairs after them.

Helena grabbed Will's coat and dragged him through the bedroom door before he took offence and dashed downstairs to thump the man, especially when she had just decided she quite liked him.

'When I want your opinion, I'll ask for it, Troughton,' Will still found the breath to yell down the stairs, even as he allowed her to tow him further into the bedroom. 'And as for you, my lady...'

'Oh, just be quiet, you,' she ordered as she slammed the door behind them and pushed him towards the grand old tester bed, so inviting-looking in the last of the light from a bank of mullioned windows.

'But...'

'Not quiet enough,' she said severely once she had him nearly where she wanted him at last and refused to let him realise she had almost lost her nerve. 'Hush,' she said as he opened his mouth to argue. She put her hand over it and felt that relentless driving need scream at the feel of it and him so close and nearly intimate as her legs threatened to let her down at the crucial moment. 'You will only try to argue me out of being me again if I let you speak,' she said and finally snatched her hand away with an effort she didn't want him to know about. She pushed at his broad chest with both hands and overbalanced him on to the bed but knew it only worked because he let her so he was at least a little bit willing to oblige her.

'At least I have finally got you at my mercy,' she murmured and dared him to even try to argue with her need to have him here in a bed with her and tangled up in passions they could embrace with years' worth of pent-up enthusiasm at long last. She needed to confirm to her own satisfaction this miracle was real and he was truly, gloriously, wonderfully alive, and maybe he needed her nearly as much as she did him.

'I want you so much, Will,' she whispered as she studied his face in the last of the daylight and felt her heart lurch with such a wide hope it frightened her. 'I have wanted you for so long and so uselessly and now I have had enough of just wanting. I am going to have you and don't you dare argue and stride about being the Major who can't trust anyone but himself to keep watch so he is too busy for a wife he has not been a proper husband to for six years, four months and five days.'

'What a memory you do have, Wife,' he murmured with a mocking look and a smug smile. 'Please don't mind me,' he said with a wolfish grin and a gesture at his prone body to say he was pretending to be at her mercy. It reminded her so much of the old days and Rake Harborough that those wretched tears pricked at her eyes once again. She fought them back since this was not the time for any more of them. Maybe it was time for her to cry with fulfilment and ecstasy, or at least she hoped so, but not for the gaps between this time and the last time they were alone in a bedroom and she was frantic for sensual satisfaction.

'You, Major, are woefully overdressed,' she informed him regally and glared down at him to say she was not charmed, but very angry he had withheld this from them for years of aching emptiness and he had better do something about it right now, and make it spectacular for her while he was about it.

'As I seem to be yours to command you might as well do something about it,' he said with a lazy, smile and a hotly inviting look.

'Oh, you would like that, wouldn't you?'

'D'you know, I rather think I would,' he said, squirming invitingly against the counterpane to say she might as well get on and undress him as not, now they were here and she had him at her mercy.

'I am not your batman,' she told him stiffly as her nerve almost failed her at the last minute. Now he was being Will the Rake before Lady Helena Snowe reformed him again—or come to think of it, did he reform her? Whatever way round it was she had waited too long for this and for so long she thought they could never do it again. So, she would not be denied because he was eyeing her so boldly it almost made her feel shy and that was ridiculous, she had never been shy with him before and it seemed stupid of her to start now.

What she had done was ache for him—for miles, hours, half a day, no, for years. It felt as if they had to confirm life itself by making love now that they had reached a sanctuary for the night and luckily his mysterious friend was not in it.

'Good, because I do not have one; I have not dared trust anyone to shave or dress and undress me for years,' he replied gruffly and began to undo his no longer pristine neckcloth with one hand while the other got busy with his ridiculously small waistcoat buttons.

'I admire your dexterity if not your economy of effort but you are going to ruin both of those if we don't divide and conquer them between us,' she told him now he had given her that confidence back somehow with that reluctant admission. She took over the buttons so he could unwind the mysteries of a man's neckcloth and save her the trouble of trying to work it out.

'I do like a nice bit of combined marital effort,' he said as if this was his idea all along and he looked as if he was thoroughly enjoying being undressed by a frantic woman.

Doubts stalked her all over again as that demon of jealousy prodded its pitchfork into her at the idea of another woman ever doing this for him. 'I believe that's what marriage is supposed to be—a joint enterprise,' she told him huffily as the last waistcoat button gave in to her impatient efforts and she eyed the flap of his riding breeches wistfully and decided it was time they did something about her layers of muslin and lawn instead.

'Here, let me,' he argued as she searched for laces and buttons and fumbled every one. 'I dreamed about doing this again so many times, Helena. I could not let myself believe it would come true again one day, but I still dreamed,' he said as if he was still half inside that dream and not quite sure this was real either.

Her heart raced with something she wasn't sure she wanted to feel again as he searched for her laces and pulled until they yielded, then he impatiently tugged them from their eyelets until her gown gaped and her fine lawn chemise did a very poor job of concealing her accelerated breathing and frantically aroused nipples from his eager gaze. Up here the sinking sun lent them a last rose-gold caress as he lost patience with that layer of drapery and tugged it off until her breasts were as naked and eager as her short corset allowed them to be.

'More layers than an onion,' he complained rather breathlessly as he tugged at the laces of that next and they yielded without much of a fight. 'Lift up, lover,' he urged and she hadn't even remembered she was still kneeling up on the bed in front of him as they both fought with their respective clothes for their freedom.

Freedom to do this, she decided hazily as she did as he bid her and raised herself far enough for him to push her remaining clothes away as quickly as possible. She purred with heady satisfaction as he spread his wonderful, broad-palmed and long-fingered hands out so he could rub her eager breasts as if he couldn't keep his hands off her now that they had a whole, dark and blissfully private night ahead of them. His murmur of sensual appreciation made her forget her qualms that she had less there than she did the last time they loved and was thinner than he probably liked a woman to be as well.

'Perfect,' he muttered as he explored her newly pared-down curves and eyed her pebble-hard, tightly furled nipples with approval.

Did he know how much she longed to feel his mouth on them again? If he did, he was dragging out the torture by licking his lips as if he was anticipating the taste of her and she had to guess what he felt now because darkness was creeping into all the corners of this grand old room and she wanted his touch so desperately. She needed her other senses to be sharp because sight was no help to her now. She wanted every moment of this loving imprinted on her memory. This was the proof she needed that he was truly here; not a dream her grieving mind made up to make the loneliness of her life without him less cruel.

'Please, Will,' she murmured as pride lost out to desperation. 'Please, put your mouth on me,' she begged and moaned as he moved his magical fingers against her in time with her accelerated breathing. 'Ah, yes, that's bliss.' She moaned as he reared up to replace his teasing fingers with his mouth and it felt as desperate for her as she was for him. She wondered if she might melt from sheer, thunderous need as sweet, hot urgency beat at the heart of her, twisted inside her so hard when he licked and suckled and praised her tight nipples with such tender, driven eagerness she felt herself getting ready to fly too soon.

Just the touch of his mouth on her bared breasts and eager nipples sent her off into an ecstasy she knew was not complete without him, but she could not hold it back for another moment. 'Oh, Will. Oh, my love…my lover!' she heard herself cry out in the throes of it and fleetingly hoped none of the men had the gall to listen at the door, or even from the bottom of the stairs as she failed to hold back a great, giveaway moan of sensual satisfaction.

Will didn't seem to care if she had given them away even more than she had already as hasty lovers who had spent far too long apart to be quiet about it now. He teased and petted and drove her on with hot and praising kisses on her needy breasts. His touch at her secret heart was a silken whisper that drove her to what seemed like the very edge of the world for a glorious moment.

'I couldn't help myself,' she apologised as soon as she came down from that first frantic peak, realising he was so intent on her pleasure he had not taken his own. 'I could not make myself wait for you,' she added with regret even as she felt the fizz and satisfaction of her own hasty climax warm her as she hadn't truly been warm since he left her asleep and searching for him in her dreams all those years ago, when he went off to war without her.

'I still have plenty of time to catch up with you, my siren,' he said unsteadily, as if he had got almost as much satisfaction from seeing her fly at his mere touch and kisses against her starving-for-him breasts as if he had flown himself. 'Better than me fading away before you got to the finish line, Helena mine,' he murmured, and he lounged back against the pillows with what she was sure would be a self-satisfied smile on his face if only she could see it.

She hadn't even realised she was still kneeling above him to present him with the best access to her blatantly begging nipples and she could already feel them peaking and hardening and rising to the temptation of more.

Helena mine, she quoted him in her head; he had not reciprocated her rash declaration with one of mutual love. She shook her head to fend off her own demons whispering that was because he didn't love her any more. Tonight it didn't matter; he was here and she loved him, had never stopped loving him and probably never would.

She tossed her head to defy a stern Fate she could feel creeping into this lovely old room with a basket of worries to lessen the sensual glory of being with her only lover again, after she had thought all hope of him was gone.

'So soft, so full of life,' Will murmured as he ran his hands through her hair, the gesture making the last of her hairpins give up their struggle to control her disobedient mane. The heavy weight of it fell around her shoulders and he rubbed a hank of it between his fingers as if he couldn't get enough of the feel of it.

'Although I loved it short, I like it even better like this,' he told her as he laid a silky strand over her skin and smoothed it out as if he loved the feel of bare skin no other man had ever seen and the silky soft hair they would never see hanging down like this either, or at least not if he had anything to do with it.

'It was easier to bundle it into a net and it costs me nothing like this,' she said as she fought for practicality against the sensuous feel of him praising her hair and her silky-feeling skin and perhaps she was still a sensual creature after all. 'Do you really like it?' she asked softly and almost despaired at her own neediness.

'I love it like this and you are a wonder, Helena—my wonder,' he whispered as he kissed the suddenly sensitive skin at the peak of her bare shoulder through her hair and made it seem wonderful to her as well. 'Now, for heaven's sake let me get these breeches off before I burst out of them to get at you.' He almost groaned the words out and she forgot her own sensual wonder long enough to touch his bare shoulders and feel him shiver with longing and need even as the longing and need inside her leapt into vital life again and she wanted him as greedily as ever.

'Hurry,' she whispered as he hastily undid buttons and pushed his close-fitting breeches off with an impatient curse. Then he shrugged off the white linen pantaloons she could just see in the summer darkness and thank goodness he had rid himself of his boots when he lay on the bed to please her—and, oh, heavens, but he did want her mightily, though, didn't he? She could feel the frantic drive of it, the hardness of his need although he wasn't currently touching her.

She caught the delicious scent of thoroughly aroused husband, not an aroused male because that would imply any other man would do for her and there was only him. So, here was her aroused, very ready to take them both up to the heavens this time, husband and what a miracle that felt like. 'I am more than ready for you, quite shamelessly ready, in fact, so stop trying to hold back in case you scare me because of the size or the need of you, Will. I want you so much; I want you urgent and hard and inside me right now.'

'Do you have any idea how desperate I am for you? If you could see me, you might quail.'

'For goodness sake, I am not a virgin. I know how you feel and need, Will, and you are my husband. I have missed you so much I can hardly stand being without you for a moment longer. So, if you won't take me right now, I shall have to take you instead,' she said and pushed him back on to the bed without even having to guess where he was exactly because she knew as if he was already a part of her again, her very present lover about to be very present inside her eager, aching-for-him sex.

Settling her knees either side of his lean hips, she didn't hesitate, but plunged down on his eager member until they were locked together again, like the desperate-for-one-another lovers they truly were. His hugely aroused shaft slid inside her wet, sleek core and she wriggled a little against the lack of him there for so long before she remembered how to stretch and luxuriate and blissfully enjoy the ultimate in pleasure between a man and a woman when the fit and feel and passion were just right and they would only ever be so with him.

'Ah, love...' She praised the feel of his hard and delicious sex inside her with infinite satisfaction as her body adapted to having her husband inside her at long last. She took his eager length and breadth and hardness fully and moaned with the sensuous pleasure of having him so high and hard there, the pleasure of it nearly joined them in ecstasy again before they had even started the long, lovely race to the ultimate satisfaction together.

No, she had to wait this time; she owed him all of it, not another side-step into her own heady climax while he looked on or tried to catch up with her and she raced ahead of all the pleasures she wanted him to have with her. She rose on the hardness and heat of him and let the rhyme and reason of lovers take over the race. Reminded of the drive to somewhere even better than she had been alone just now, she rose and fell as he kissed and cupped and cradled and licked her with his deliciously roughened rider's hands and wickedly knowing tongue.

His kiss, when he finally captured her mouth in the midst of their preoccupied race to the finish line, took over the drive and desperation from her. His frantic, praising tongue echoed the movements of their joined bodies and took it deeper and needier while he used his hands on her slender backside to settle their rhythm to a headier pace and he drove deeper than she thought he could. She felt the heat and shock and sheer delight of his climax striving deep and heavy inside her and suddenly they were both there and she bowed and writhed in time to his convulsions of ecstasy, felt his release even as her eyes rolled back in the absolute pleasure and fulfilment of it. He drove her up even higher into pleasure than he ever had before.

She felt as if they were giving each other all the feeling and closeness and neediness they had not been able to say yet; all they had lost for so long in one endless, glorious consummation that said everything they did not have words for. They flew over his careful barriers, over the dark thoughts unwilling to let her inside them, and reached out and remade complete intimacy. This loving felt so important, so crucial to her she revelled in every last driven convulsion of sated pleasure.

Now try to tell me you don't love me, you idiot, her inner siren whispered as she kissed his bare shoulder.

She loved the feel of his hair-roughened torso brushing against her now even more sensitised nipples and breasts heaving with the effort and pleasure of what they had just done together as she sank down on to him and sighed with delight and contentment. They were right again, as a deeply loving man with his desperately-in-love-with-him wife. Here in the intimate darkness of a strange bedchamber they were Helena and Will the lovers again and never mind the treachery and betrayals and intrigue that might be waiting for them outside. This was where they belonged, it was their kingdom.

Chapter Eleven

Will awoke to another fine August morning and could instantly tell that it was already too late for the early start he had promised himself they would make last night. The sun was lighting up an old armchair through the opposite bank of leaded windows from the ones that had lit Helena so seductively in the last rosy rays of the sunset last night as she more or less commanded him to make love to her and never mind dinner or anything else.

He recalled his pleasure with a wolfish grin and his mind went hazy again with sumptuous memories of her tangling up his senses over and over again until he hardly knew where he left off and she began. An image of his wife in extremis threatened to fog his mind as well as his vision again, but that simply would not do in full daylight. He blinked to remind himself it was late and too much of the day had already been wasted. Precious hours had flitted past while he lay sated for now and simply sleeping with his wife in his arms, dreaming of love instead of war for once.

The angle of that curious sun scolded him for such a lazy time of day to be waking up. High time he was busy keeping his wife alive and never mind well and truly loved. He bit back a fierce curse at his tardiness because he still didn't dare to rouse the siren at his side because then they might waste a good deal more if he did and to hell with the killer on his track and everything else as well.

Even so, he could not help himself glancing at her asleep at his side and then he got distracted, wondering why he had thought she was too thin when he first set eyes on her again. Shock, he supposed. He had been so stupidly surprised she had changed from the bold and lusty bride he remembered and a much more honed and self-contained lady stood brazenly in Lady Helena's shoes six and a half years on. Yes, she had changed and why hadn't he expected it after all he and her family had put her through since last time they loved together?

This Helena was not as radiant and eagerly youthful as the daring society lady he remembered, but she was deeper and perhaps even truer to herself than she had been back then. He smiled at the thought of that Helena— bold and bad as she thought herself when they loved beyond reason without benefit of clergy the first time. He supposed he had expected her to be frozen in time after their wedding and furtive honeymoon and of course she had to disoblige him. She had had to go on with her life without him and he felt even more of a fool for thinking she would be exactly as he remembered her now.

He lay marvelling at the slender curves on show; she must have kicked the sheet off during the night. He wanted to wake her with a needy kiss or a wandering touch, then whisper caresses over her body so he could explore her delightful curves by daylight to add even more to his fascination with his wife as she really was. She was perfect as she was, he decided, although if she lost even one more ounce she really would be too thin. He already knew her narrow waist and gently rounded feminine bottom fitted his large masculine hands so perfectly his manhood went rigid with hungry appreciation and wicked intent just thinking about putting them there again.

As for her breasts, exactly the right size to be cupped in a delighted husband's hands, and her sweetly peaked rosy-amber nipples, he gazed at them and decided they were perfection—always had been, always would be. He remembered how they tasted, then and now: scented with pure essence of Helena, her unique womanly scent enhanced by rosewater and a hint of clean linen—plus desire, he recalled as a yearning to lick them into aroused urgency right now nearly overcame him. There simply wasn't time for a repeat of last night's wondrous performance and encores, or was there?

He felt torn between his duty to protect her from the silent avenger who had stalked him for so long and this desperate longing to make love to his wife until they both forgot their long and bitter years apart. Will the Lover wanted to lie here and watch her sleep as the day built up into late summer heat and they tumbled into lazy lovings one after the other until the day was spent…just like a very crucial but wilfully disobedient part of him might be at last by the end of all that hot and hasty self-indulgence, he decided dreamily.

Soon even Helena would be too hot for sleep any longer, though, so he had to get out of bed before she opened her sleepy eyes and they fell into that lusty day instead of pressing on to as much safety as he could dare hope for until he caught the cur after him and handed him to the authorities. Even the thought of reaching over and waking Helena with a kiss on her temptingly parted lush mouth had him so aroused he wasn't sure he could be anything but clumsy if he tried to walk away from her before she woke up now. He was ridiculously satisfied to know he was the reason she was so exhausted she had slept on long after the time he was sure she usually sprang out of bed to chivvy the world into submission.

It worked both ways, though, and he knew he could not stop at kissing; he hadn't three times in the night when one of them woke the other because there was no point wasting all that lovely darkness. When they had lost so many nights together already, no wonder they were frantic. For a few self-indulgent moments he allowed himself the sheer luxury of gazing at his wife without her perceptive grey gaze staring back at him as if she was determined to read his mind and get all the way down to his grubby soul if she could manage it.

He was supposed to be protecting her, though, wasn't he? He felt very reluctant to die today, so, if he did want to protect her from this beast trying to kill them, and he very definitely did, it seemed like a good idea for him to survive as well. And that was what loving Helena did to him, it made life not just worthwhile, but sharp and clean again—newly minted.

No, it wasn't loving, it was need; he couldn't admit to loving her even in the privacy of his own head until she was safe and they stood some chance of owning a future together that was longer than a few hours or days. He had put her at too much risk by loving her once upon a time and promised himself not to do it again until the threat he had lived with for so long was gone, or he was.

That reminded him—he was not supposed

to risk getting her with child until he had done so.

Failed again, Harborough.

He felt that failure jar right through him and take the shine off the possibility of enjoying the rest of the morning making love when their sated sleep had already stolen so much of it. She was too much temptation for his self-control to stand much longer. There was too much haste and heat and glory between them to play the gallant husband and withdraw before he spent himself inside her, he recalled with a tomcat grin it was as well neither of them could see.

Fancy her marching him upstairs as soon as they got here and refusing to take no for an answer like that. And he did fancy it; would always fancy it while there was breath in his body. She was still his impulsive, passionate, Helena at heart and never mind the changes he and time had wrought. His wife was herself and so fully alive and demandingly irresistible under the dull layers and tugged-back hairstyle and the newly slender lines of her delicious body.

Despite the worry heavy on his shoulders

and the dread waiting to ice at his heart when he was his usual self again, he felt as if there was far more of him alive this morning than there had been for a very long time. Probably since the last time he woke up in bed with his wife beside him and watched her sleep. Except that last time he was too much of a coward to face her bravely blinked back tears as he walked away, so he had sneaked out of their bed before she was awake. She had not stirred then as he left her to do his duty, or at least that was what he'd thought it was at the time. Now he wasn't sure that his country would not have done just as well without him.

So, why the devil *did* the deluded young idiot leave his wife of one week alone to face any consequences of their driven loving? What stupid maggot had got into his head to make him think Wellington could not defeat Joseph Bonaparte—the supposed King of Spain—perfectly well without any help from such a junior officer?

Arrogant young fool, he condemned his younger self now. He should have sold out the moment he contemplated marriage with elusive, picky Lady Helena Snowe, who was neither of those things to the lucky young dog who fell head over ears in love with her the moment he set eyes on her. By then he had served eight years in the Army, as the only thing his father had ever done for his son before he died was buy Will a pair of colours for his sixteenth birthday.

Captain Harborough should already have been cured of heroism by the time he met Helena. He had been wounded more than once in the service of his country and seen the chaos of the ill-fated Walcheren Expedition as well as that harsh retreat to Corunna, but, no, he was far too self-important to realise one ignorant young idiot more or less would make no difference to the outcome of a long and bloody war.

With hindsight he knew all a good officer could do was keep as many of his men alive as possible and take the fight to the enemy when ordered. The rest depended on the general in charge of the battle and the Duke of Wellington could be harsh and cold, but he was a damned good one and extraordinarily good at deploying his troops to the maximum advantage. Then Will was forced to find out how not to be a good officer any more and become a cunning spy and at least thinking of the grim truth behind his lies had stopped him being so rampantly needy for the unique woman at his side.

Now he could slide quietly out of my lady's bed again without stumbling, he paused to slip on his breeches so he did not terrify any maids lurking about the place, but he merely picked up the rest of his scattered clothes, grinning at the sight of his shirt draped over an ancient oak coffer like a flag of surrender. Surrender to bliss and my lady's demands, he recalled with an even wider grin, then made himself pad out on bare feet so he did not wake her. Stopping to retrieve his riding boots from opposite corners of the room would be folly right now and he could borrow anything else he needed until she was safely awake and abroad again.

Grey was right—he probably did owe Will a safe place to stay *and* a few items of his clothing for luring a friend into his shadowy trade when he was almost innocent, even if he didn't think he was at the time.

'Where is my husband?' Helena asked the maid who came to answer the bell.

'The gentleman said he was going to inspect the horses, ma'am.'

'Oh, thank you.' Helena felt silly for panicking and of course he could only have been gone for a few minutes. The rumpled sheets still held a hint of his warmth and even Will could not get into trouble that quickly without her. The scent of him lingered in this lovely old bed as well, she realised with an appreciative sniff, and the delicious memory of sated male and his delighted wife made her smile like a siren. Still, it was high time she got up and faced the world again. 'I would like hot water and my valise, please.'

'Yes, madam,' the girl said and somehow managed not to look avidly curious about such odd visitors.

This fine old house must belong to a gentleman of means, Helena thought as she waited for that hot water and eyed the polished oak panelling and sparkling diamond-paned windows. The house was clean and cared for, but had none of the carefully chosen touches of colour and interesting objects to say it was a cherished home. She wondered why Will's mysterious spymaster and so-called friend pursued such a shady career if he had all this to come home to. Perhaps he didn't, perhaps he had used his secretive connections to acquire the means to buy this ancient manor. Not that it mattered how he got it, but she was more certain than ever Will trusted nobody else but his uncle and the two men who had kept his secret for so long. This place must belong to the man responsible for that secret being so cruel and enduring and so very, very useful to the man who lured him into it as if he was doing Will a favour.

She should spring out of bed and refuse to owe one more lazy moment or even a crumb of breakfast to the man, but didn't see the point in cutting off her nose to spite her face. It would look odd if she stormed off into the sunlight, refusing to take a morsel of the man's bread when he wasn't even here to be insulted. She reminded herself every hour she and Will spent together would make them stronger.

They certainly only had eyes for one another last night, she recalled with a reminiscent smile at one boot in one corner of the room and the other askew on the opposite side of it. They had thrown their clothes off to be naked together as fast as possible and whatever changes they had undergone during six and a half years of weary absence, the passionate need to make love to one another with driven urgency had not faded.

Should she worry her husband was striding about the place without his boots? No, if she worried about him whenever he was out of sight their marriage would never reach the deep mutual contentment she longed for. After the ghastly void of thinking he was gone from her life for ever they must savour every moment together. The threat that held Will in limbo for so long needed to be undone before they were truly free. Then they could get back to the important business of learning to live together properly, or improperly, for the rest of their lives.

She shivered at the grim thought of having to live without Will ever again and hurried to wash and dress and put up her hair. Despite the softness in her eyes and the kiss-softened mouth, the Helena Will first fell in love with was only a memory now. She stared at the austere woman in the mirror almost as if she was looking at a stranger. Will had certainly aged far more than his years since they parted, but she had as well.

Yet when she looked closer, she realised she did look younger this morning than she did yesterday, when she woke up thinking it was just one more day. To survive life without him, she had had to close off an essential part of herself the day she heard of Will's death in battle, so she hid the vibrant young woman who loved him so much.

But now the old Helena was peeping out from behind the disguise. She wanted her blind trust in a rosy future back. It might never be truly as blind as it was back then, but it could still be rich with wonders and so very promising, if the gap of Will trusting his friend when she was so suspicious of the man could be bridged. Will had lived such a hard, closed-in life for the last few years, but he was still there under the shell he had grown to protect himself and so she would let him carry her off somewhere he thought was safe where they could build a day-to-day intimacy they had never had before.

Chapter Twelve

'I think we should ride today,' Helena said airily when they were eating a belated breakfast.

Will wondered how she had managed to lose weight rather than put it on while they were apart, but a very pleasant reverie about why she was so hungry now would not get them any further on today and they must not run back upstairs to luxuriate in my lady's borrowed bed until it was too late for them to go anywhere at all. 'I'm not sure they have a fast enough cart horse in the stables,' he teased her.

'Beast,' she said, 'I am very hungry.'

'I know,' he replied with a reminiscent grin. 'For food.'

'That as well? What vast appetites you have nowadays, my lady.'

'I have always had them,' she told him rather crossly and he felt a sharp pang of jealousy at the thought of her ever indulging them with another man. That was the reason for half the grey hairs he had acquired since they last broke their fast together on a lazy morning after making love until the stars faded from the sky.

He glared at his plate until he could see past the nasty haze of envy and hatred for a man who did not exist. If Helena said she had spent the last six and a half years sleeping alone then that was what she had done. Many women would have quietly mourned their secret husband, then shrugged and taken their happiness elsewhere, but Lady Helena Snowe was not a run-of-the-mill kind of female and he was guiltily glad she had held fast to their love even after she'd thought he was dead.

'I know,' he said and his smile grew into a wolfish, reminiscent grin at the thought of her demanding sensual satisfaction last night, as if years of frustration needed sating urgently and frequently and he was certainly game to try, once they were safely in his own secluded lair.

'Since we first set eyes on each other anyway,' she qualified.

'I know,' he said again. 'I am not used to sharing. No, not you—words,' he added hastily. 'I learned to keep even my thoughts so close I seem to have lost the ability to tell you about them.'

'I don't need words,' she told him with a long and not very cool look that said they had communicated very well last night without very much said.

'You still deserve them and I promise to keep searching for the right ones and find a way to say them to you.'

'When all this is over?'

He nodded because he had made himself that stupid vow not to tell her he loved her again until he knew they were both safe and looking forward to however long they had on earth together without this nagging fear his nemesis would find a way to destroy him through her.

'After so long pretending to be dead, how can you refuse to live as best you can now that we are alive again together?' she said quietly and her words went to his heart like an arrow to the gold.

'Because when you are officially a dead man even hope feels like a self-inflicted cruelty,' he said as if the words were being ripped out of him. 'Being less than nobody and knowing what I had done to you with that last lie raked at my soul like a cat-o'-nine-tails, Helena. I made myself live only for what came next until I was dead inside; I became whoever I was supposed to be at the time and lived his life instead of mine. When you don't exist, there's no point hoping for more and I knew what I did to you was unforgivable so there was no point in me doing it anyway.'

'We shall have to see about that and for a man who says he has no words you seem remarkably good at picking them,' she said calmly and ate another bite as if they were merely discussing the weather. If not for the faint shake in her hand as she raised a slice of toast to her mouth and a swiftly controlled wobble of her lush lips before she bit into it, he could almost think her unmoved by his rare eloquence.

'Somehow, I say things to you I promised myself I would never say to anyone. Yet I don't want you to feel weighed down by things I have done and seen without you, Helena. How can I live with you day after day, make love to you and be your undeserving husband and lover knowing I have broken an essential part of you? If I told you what I really did when we were apart it would sicken you and I did you a huge wrong when I pretended to be dead for so long. Maybe we would do better apart when I know you are safe and this devil has been dealt with. I have been a coward since the day we met and I'm not much better now.'

And how did they go from a lovely bubble of light and laughter after a wondrous night of shared pleasure to this? His memories of her made his world seem sane when it was so mired in blood and betrayal, he didn't even want to remember who he was any more. Yet he had made her lie and say she was Lady Helena Snowe and not his wife for so long—how could she truly forgive him?

'You are not getting away from me that easily, William Harborough,' she argued with a militant glint in her fine grey eyes that almost gave him back the hope he had just warned her not to have.

Her belief in him was a huge gift, he realised, and, as always, she had given it freely and without strings. He nearly choked on his own toast as he took a bite to hide the way his own lips shook at the unevenness of her wholehearted generosity and his empty cynicism.

'Here—you might as well have my tea to wash it down,' she said, eyeing the pitiful spectacle he must be with his streaming eyes and a cough he struggled to overcome. 'Better?' she said when he finally sat back and did as she bid with a grimace at the taste.

'Much,' he said huskily, then reached for the coffee pot. 'I seem to have lost the taste for tea with my true identity,' he explained hoarsely, the excuse of that coughing bout yet another lie.

'I'm sure you were only used to the finest coffee when you lived in Spain,' she said as if she knew perfectly well he was not.

'I certainly wasn't, but things taste even more delicious after you live without them for so long.'

'I suppose they do,' she said with a bold, smug look and somehow neither of them was talking about coffee and tea any more.

'And I do have a taste for the real thing,' he said and it was true.

Every time he saw the lure to intimacy in a potential lover's eyes, he would allow himself to remember he was married to a far finer woman to hold back his eagerness for the sheer, blind relief of sex with a willing woman and shake his head regretfully. But remembering her left him so torn apart by jealousy of some damn rogue she could be loving instead of him he would have to slam the door on his memories again to keep himself sane.

'I agree,' she said quietly.

About what?

Ah, yes, coffee and pale imitations fading next to the luxurious reality.

'I have only ever loved you, Will; I shall only ever love you,' she said in case he was too obtuse to read her meaning.

'And I have not loved another woman since I met you,' he said like a weasel-tongued politician sliding all around the truth.

Why couldn't he just say it? Why make

her stare at him as if she was trying to decide which species he was? He could tell her what she wanted to hear, watch the tension fade from her lush, kiss-stung mouth until she smiled at him with all the love she still wanted to feel for him in her eyes. He was not the man she had loved any more though, was he? And now she was glaring at him with narrowed eyes as if he had stolen the family silver and kicked the cat on the way out.

'Well, lucky me,' she said sarcastically.

He had to stare through the window behind her to stop himself leaping to his feet and kissing her breathless before he carried her back up the stairs to take up where they left off with the dawn. He suppressed a groan and knew today was going to be the start of his constant battle between the lure of sensuous satisfaction with his wife whenever they could grab it and his iron determination to keep her safe.

'Why do you want to ride?' he asked, his voice husky as a double meaning sent a surge of unwanted arousal through his unruly body again. He took another sip of coffee to let her think he was still recovering from his choking fit even as his rigidly eager little man screamed *Liar!*

'Because it's less predictable to ride across country rather than sit in your uncle's curricle waiting to be shot at,' she said bluntly and he shuddered.

'You would be an easier mark riding across a field or through a dark wood than in a fast-moving carriage.'

'Only if your enemy knew which field or wood to look in and how can they know that when even I don't know where we are going? No doubt you told Edward and you made sure nobody was on our tail all the way here. I know this house is safe as, well, houses I suppose, or you would never have brought me here, but even though I didn't ask you a lot of questions that doesn't mean I'm not thinking them. In the end, I decided you probably know what you are doing and arguing would only slow us down.'

'Only probably?'

'Well, you did stay away for years and pretend you were dead; you can hardly expect my unqualified faith until you prove you deserve it.'

'How much more proof do you need, woman?' he said with a mock leer.

'That's not the sort of proof I meant,' she said primly.

It was no good; he just had to laugh at an expression of bemused disapproval she must have learned from her mother. A deep chuckle turned into open laughter when she stared at him as if he had run mad. It felt so good to laugh freely again so he grinned to invite her to see the funny side of her being shocked at anything he did after the night of rampant passion they had just shared.

'Although I suppose I could be open to persuasion,' she added throatily and wrong-footed him yet again.

'Behave yourself, woman,' he said. 'If you really want to ride, we might as well, but let's have no more argument until we are safely where we need to be.'

'Are you ever going to tell me where that is?' she asked and the mischief left her lovely grey eyes until he could not read them. His lies had turned her into a woman who could hide her thoughts and feelings behind a bland mask and what a bitter lesson it looked from here.

'Somewhere safe,' he replied all the same.

'Where you can leave me while you put the world to rights for me?'

'What else can I do?' he said and she turned her head away as if he had disappointed her yet again.

'Then I prefer to ride. How long before we can leave?'

'Twenty minutes to pick a good mount and have a side-saddle put on it and make sure you pack enough for a few days on the road just in case we get delayed.'

'Very well,' she said and he felt on the outside of her life again and it felt so wrong after the night they had just shared.

In fact, the last five years had never felt more wrong than they did when he made his way out to Grey's stables to find a suitable mount for a lady.

After hastily donning her sister-in-law's favourite habit, Helena tracked down Troughton, the unlikely butler, to persuade him to deliver her letter to his master. 'And please don't pretend you have no idea where he is because I am not such a flat I will believe you,' she added when he looked blank.

'I might know where to start looking for him.'

'Excellent,' she said and gave him a guinea.

She had to trust the man would do as he said as hastily as possible and suddenly she wanted to be gone from this fine old house that felt as if it had an absence at the heart of it rather than a presence. She shivered and wondered how she could distrust a man she had never met so much. Will seemed blind to the wrongness at the heart of this whole business and she felt guilty hoping his mysterious friend was as false as she thought he was, because if she was wrong the monster on Will's tail could be real.

Chapter Thirteen

Will was thinking his way around her feminine weaknesses again and Helena clenched the reins in her fists, then made herself relax because her tension would transmit to her horse if she wasn't careful. They might as well have stayed in the curricle all the way to his mystery destination since he kept to a steady trot and opened gates for her to ride through rather than having them jump them. It was driving her demented.

For a while she had endured it because it seemed to make him feel better, but now that they were near the hottest part of the day he had slowed their pace even further and seemed intent on seeking out cooling patches of woodland for them to saunter through as if they had all day. She wanted this journey to wherever he thought he could hide her safely over.

They had a marriage to rebuild and so much to learn about one another and she was determined not to be left there until called for. It wrung her heart he was so haunted by his fear she might be attacked at any moment, but pity didn't change things. She concentrated on her hurry to make up for five years of heartbreak and separation in one another's arms instead. That was an excellent reason to get wherever they were going as rapidly as possible.

'We should stop for lunch now, so you can rest during the heat of the day,' Will said when they reached the next copse and he turned his horse towards the stream at the heart of it as if that was the only sensible idea available.

'I have spent day after day in the saddle riding around my brother's estates after my father died. I am not a shy little violet who can only bloom in the shade or whatever frail flower you think of next. I have ridden hard, walked far and climbed and scrambled and trudged over much worse ground than this all day, then done it again the next day and the day after that, week after week, year after year while you were gone.'

'Admirable,' he said so calmly she wanted to hit him. 'It begs the question of what your brother was doing while you were working so hard, but why would that résumé be of interest to me right now?'

'Stop playing the weary and superior aristocrat; I can outdo you at it any day I choose to and criticising my brother will not make me so angry I forget what we are arguing about. Edward was doing the same on other parts of the estates so we would not be declared bankrupt and thrown on the mercy of the parish. My brother's acres are too vast for him to deal with alone and there was no money for land agents or bailiffs.'

And I was so glad not to sit at home mourning you day after weary day, she thought but did not say.

'And?'

'And what, you infuriating man?'

'Why do those hardships alter how I should treat my wife?'

'Because I don't need fussing over; I can ride as fast and as far as you can if necessary

and we can't go on ambling about the countryside like a pair of Bath breakdowns. We
need to be wherever you won't tell me we are
bound for before we are caught in the open by
this enemy you are so convinced is hunting
us down like vermin.'

'I don't think it, I *know*,' he said dourly.

'Then go faster, Will. Get us where we are
going in good time to shore up your defences.
That is what we're supposed to be doing, isn't
it? Going from one safe place to another?'

'Aye,' he said wearily and now she felt
guilty.

If the idea of them being so vulnerable in
the open wouldn't horrify him so much she
might suggest a better diversion by this sleepy
stream in the middle of nowhere to distract
him from fears she still thought were probably unfounded. 'Then treat me as your ally
instead of an encumbrance, Will. Sauntering
around the countryside as if we have all the
time in the world like this is beyond absurd.'

'What do you have in mind?'

'For us to ride hard and keep on doing so
until we get where we are going, instead of
acting as if we are on a royal progress with

prearranged stops for the night and all the luxuries I simply do not need waiting for us along the way.'

'You want to ride day and night until we get there?' he said as if it was such an unthinkable idea he was about to laugh at it.

'Yes, if we can, although I don't know if we need to do so since you refuse to tell me where we are going. I don't see why you cannot at least say how long it should take us to get there.'

'The day after tomorrow.'

'At your pace or mine?'

'Mine,' he admitted with a tight look she was becoming a little too familiar with.

'Make it tomorrow instead,' she demanded. 'It's ridiculous for us to take longer than we need if we don't have to.'

'Tearing across the country would attract attention,' he argued.

'Why?'

'Ladies don't gallop hell for leather as if they are doing it for a bet.'

'No, but young gentlemen do,' she said and the idea made so much sense she didn't know why she hadn't thought of it earlier.

'Oh, no, don't even ask me to dress you up as a boy and watch you ride astride all the way.'

'All right, then, I won't,' she said and dug her heel into her mount's side to hurry him into a canter.

'Where are you going?' Will demanded.

'To find the nearest town where I can buy an outfit for my ragtag little brother who hates being fitted for clothes and will have to put up with whatever I go home with since we are about the same height at this stage in his rascally young life.'

'And a man's saddle as well?'

'No, you can do that. I thought spies were supposed to be resourceful.'

'Not spies, intelligence officers,' he said testily, but increased his snail's pace to keep up and glared at her instead of fixing his stubborn gaze between his horse's ears. That was progress, wasn't it?'

'I must say I can't see much sign of it at the moment,' she muttered, but knew he had heard her.

'Well, if that's what you insist on wanting, I shall have to restore your faith in me,' he said with a look of such saintly resignation she eyed him suspiciously.

'You will get me clothes to fit a young lad and a man's saddle, then?'

'Trust me,' he demanded and she wasn't at all sure she did as they rode much faster towards the nearest place where he could hide her while he got on with whatever he needed to do to hide their tracks and get away a lot faster than they were now.

'I suppose you think this is funny?' Helena asked the not very gentlemanly figure ahead of her riding a brutish-looking horse that tried to nip her shaggy pony whenever it was close enough.

'I do, actually,' Will said with a sidelong glance to say she had what she wanted so what was she complaining about?

'Shame on you, then,' she said with a furious frown.

'Why? I could be ashamed of the ragbag urchin who refuses to ride several yards behind his master as an apprentice should, I suppose. Not that you seem at all grateful for the privilege of riding alongside me whenever the path allows it.'

'Why should I be when you found me a pony, not a horse, and guyed me up in the sort of rags I would not even expect a stable boy to wear at Hawley.'

'They are very clean rags and at least nobody will mistake you for a fine lady in them.'

'Not even you,' she said darkly and refused to see the funny side.

'I still might, if not for your foul tongue and worse temper. No apprentice would dare say the things you do to your master.'

'Then bad cess to you, Mr Whoever You Are.'

'Best save your breath because you are the one who wanted to gallop into the hills with me and to forget being considered or cared for and that's almost what we're doing now, bar the galloping. I never met a woman less satisfied with getting her own way than you are right now, Wife.'

'This isn't what I meant; we will get wherever we are going no faster than we would have done your way going at this rate, *Husband*.'

He made a furtive survey of the treeless mountainside in case there was a hawk or sheep listening with malicious intent and Helena rolled her eyes to tell him not to be such an idiot.

'This is a much shorter route, but don't blame me because it is also a rougher one,' he said dourly. 'You insisted you were up for any adventure I cared to throw at you so you can hardly complain that I took you at your word.'

'Oh, can't I?' she mumbled resentfully, then had to resort to frowning at his broad back when she was forced to do what a humble apprentice rogue should and fall back on the narrowing path and follow her supposed master.

At least she could glower at him in peace now and gloomily take in the rugged scenery around them. She might do that since straight ahead of her was a fine view of Will's bad-tempered but strong mount's rump and she would have to crick her neck if she wanted to stare at Will's ramshackle figure instead. He was right about one thing, thank goodness—her much-washed shirt and jerkin did not seem to be harbouring unwanted visitors. So, at least she wasn't uncomfortable from insect bites as well, but the bindings he had insisted she wear to suppress her breasts, despite her protests they hardly needed it, were quite irksome enough on their own.

Will had insisted if she wanted to leave the coat of her ragged ensemble off, she must conceal her feminine assets from any fellow wanderers they happened to meet and it was still a hot day so of course she had to agree, but they were one more reason to feel hot and frustrated and out of sorts as she watched Will sway to the shaggy cob's motion as if he was quite comfortable ambling along in the middle of nowhere.

The road had become more like a rarely used path and they travelled quite a long way without her even noticing as she chewed over her grievances in resentful silence. They had been climbing steadily for some time, she realised, and began to appreciate her sturdy pony instead of cursing Will for putting her on such a humble mount to humble *her*. At least they were not already settled for the night in some fine nest he thought would hold her safe and pampered until they could resume their stately progress. She supposed that was a victory of a kind.

She eyed the steep slope ahead and the one already behind them and it didn't feel like a win. It felt as if they were wandering in a wilderness where only Will's wits and natural arrogance would keep the wolves at bay. Wolves were extinct in Britain, she reminded herself as a superstitious shiver iced down her back and she half expected to hear the uncanny howl of one over the horizon in the almost twilight gloom all the same.

'When will we be in Wales?' she asked.

'We are already,' he said and kept his attention on finding a path that would not leave them outlined against the setting sun longer than necessary as they crossed the horizon.

His ingrained caution worried her because how was a man like him ever going to settle back into a mundane everyday sort of life as heir to Lord Flamington now? Will was so used to such danger and excitement even the challenges he would face as the future master of Deepdale would seem humdrum. She had never wanted to be a future countess for him to feel half-hearted about having at his side either. She had never wanted to be a countess at all if it came to that, just Will's everyday sort of Army wife and she was never going to be that now.

'Why Wales?' she asked to keep her depressing ideas at bay.

'Because it's beautiful and I thought you might like it?'

'Be serious, Major Harborough,' she said sternly and he glared at her before surveying the barren hillside for potential enemies again and that little worm of doubt about him being content with a mundane life after this one squirmed a little harder.

'I have a house about twenty miles from here as the crow flies and set in a valley where I will soon know if a stranger comes anywhere near us,' he told her impatiently.

'You never mentioned it to me in the old days.'

'We were busy,' he said so shortly she knew she was close to secrets he had always kept from her, even before the biggest one of all, that he was still alive.

She felt as if her cherished story of how they were back then was turning into fiction in front of her nose. Captain Will and Lady Helena were so deep in love, it went; so completely, ridiculously and instantly in love they could not help themselves taking that love to the logical conclusion and then marrying one another so they could do it all again with benefit of clergy.

Now it seemed as if his side of that love was always not quite the everything she had once thought it was. Will had a house up ahead of them, hidden away in a secret valley. Maybe he cherished it too much to tell her about it and never mind him being too busy loving her before he left for the wars to tell her about it. Perhaps the place was too important to him to reveal it to his smitten bride, even with love and lust so hot and heady between them they were constantly being carried away by it.

For the first time the lovely unity she had believed in for so long felt as fragile as a cobweb on an autumn morning: beautiful and intricate and strong, but at the same time so gossamer fine that a careless gesture could destroy it. She shivered in the heavy evening shadows on this eastern side of the mountain and her pony shook his shaggy head and snorted as if he had picked up on her unease.

'How will you know if someone is coming after us in your secret eyrie?' she made herself ask him despite the fact most of her mind was worrying at a very different question. 'Is it a fairy kingdom? Do you have magical ears and eyes behind every tree and rock?'

She thought this place might prove to be the death of her last illusion that he loved her as completely as she did him, but she doubted very much it was a magical fiefdom ruled over by a half-human, half-magical master. Although come to think about it, he had cast a spell over her from the first instant they laid eyes on one another, but that was love and lust, not an otherworldly enchantment.

'Just human curiosity and a remote neighbourhood,' he said with an impatient look behind them and another at the almost setting sun as they finally reached the peak of this hill or mountain or whatever it was. 'Given your almost mythically superb horsemanship and self-proclaimed stamina, do you think you could hurry yourself a little so that we can reach a safer place to camp overnight than the side of a bare mountain, my hell-born brat?'

'Don't call me that.'

'I can hardly call you Helena when you're guyed up like that.'

'I don't see why not.'

'The first rule of spying is never to give anything away that you don't have to.'

'I thought you were an intelligence officer and anyway there's nobody else up here to give it away to,' she argued sulkily.

'Sound travels easily across apparently empty places, especially at night.'

'Then stop talking.'

'You started it.'

'Did not.'

'Did too.'

And that did it; she had to chuckle as they argued about nothing at all. The wretch always did have a way of quirking one wicked eyebrow at her and defusing her fury in an infuriating instant. The threatened tear in her dearest dream mended itself as she realised he was already more like the Will she once knew and loved so much. The frigid stranger who had turned around to face her with such a blank gaze only yesterday was already fading into his harsh past.

It was his armour, she realised. He had thought she was sure to reject him after his determined lies, would refuse to have anything more to do with him for deceiving her so grievously and for so very long. Somehow *his* uncertainty made hers feel ridiculous, because if he was indifferent to her how could she hurt him? And they had always lived their lives together at the gallop, hadn't they? High time they got to know one another better and deeper and maybe then they could trust their love through the harshest of trials—such as the one he had already been through without her.

Even with that encouraging idea lingering in her head she had spare time to be astonished at how long the twilight could last up here in this cool, clear summer air at this time of year on a bare Welsh mountainside. By Helena's reckoning, since Will had traded in his fine gold watch for her not very fine clothes and these unassuming horses, half an hour had passed in silence after he said she was making too much noise. It was a matter of pride not to ask any more questions or even grunt when the path was too steep to burden the horses and she stubbed her toe on a raised stone since it was too dark to see it.

She would not give him a chance to accuse her of slowing them down or making him stop for the night before he was ready, not after making such a fuss about being used to riding all day, every day. She bit back a gasp as her toe throbbed painfully and he was too busy straining his senses to probe the rapidly falling darkness to even notice when she flailed her arms for balance. She told herself the worst of the pain would soon recede and she really was not a weak and demanding female, but a little concern for her well-being on this ever-darkening path would have been nice.

Determined not to limp or gasp out loud, she had to bite back a sigh of relief when Will and his now quietly plodding horse finally led the way into a shallow valley full of the even deeper shadows of stunted thorn trees on the sunset side of the mountain, where a few last glimmers of daylight let her pick out sky from shadows before darkness finally fell.

'Yes, I thought this place might do,' Will said so softly she felt prickles at the back of her neck as the small hairs raised in warning that there could be listening ears out there, although she still didn't think they had been followed.

There were still plenty of hardy rogues intent on taking what they could from unwary travellers who had to sleep some time, but Will was probably always alert for danger now so that would be nothing out of the ordinary for him. She shivered at the thought of the stealthy, always guarded life he had been forced to live for the last five years and the movement made her aware of those wretched bandages binding her breasts once again. She sighed, suspecting she was stuck with the dratted things for however long it would take them to get to his mysterious Welsh refuge.

She diverted herself from the ache in her abused toe and the discomfort of those bandages by wondering what his house was like. It seemed likely it came to him through the female line since magnificent Deepdale ran in his male one. It could be a manor or a farmhouse on a lady's dower lands and if things had been different maybe Helena could have lived in it, if only she had known Will owned it and his family thought she had a right to.

It could have been her sanctuary from prying eyes and gossip; she could have lived there cushioned by memories of Will at every turn to make the place seem ever dearer. As his official wife and widow she would have been entitled to live there, but maybe he wanted it for someone else.

Stop it, she ordered herself as tiredness and a hint of betrayal left the bitter taste of jealousy in her mouth again.

Yet another important fact your husband decided you didn't need to know, a sneaky little worm of doubt whispered in her ear.

But she would refuse to listen to it. Both their lives were very different now and that was enough for her to be going on with.

'We can't light a fire as it might be seen from too far away or someone could smell smoke drifting down from somewhere it should not be,' Will whispered as he led his horse through a crumbling archway and she sensed as much as saw a lofty ruin arch over their heads where the darkness seemed even darker here and there.

'As well it's high summer and not that cold, then,' she replied stoically and supposed if it was a ruined chapel or even a remote abbey it would feel like sacrilege to light a fire in here anyway.

'And at least it's not raining for once,' he said with a smile in his voice that made her long for everything she knew they could not have here. Even if they were not this weary and virtually in the open, Will would think it was far too risky for them to forget the rest of the world in one another's arms tonight and she knew this was no place for such things even if they weren't in danger of being discovered.

'Spoken like a true Welshman,' she tried to joke and stop herself longing for him to take her in his arms and love her anyway.

'If I was, I would say it in Welsh...but I can only remember a few words.'

'If you had ever truly lived here, you would know it. So, are you ever going to tell me who left you this house we are heading for and why you have never told me about it?'

'It is my great-grandmother's house and when I was a very small boy she would tear herself away from it and visit Deepdale for a month or so at a time and sing me to sleep in her own language. I suppose that must have been during times when my Spanish grandmother was elsewhere or too busy ruling the roost to croon at me in *her* mother tongue.'

'You seem to have heard a mixture of languages from the cradle; no wonder you grew up with a knack for picking them up. I do envy you.'

'Do you? It's proved something of a double-edged sword to me.'

'It must have been if that's why you became an intelligence officer in the first place,' she said as nonchalantly as she could, but he refused to take the bait and tell her more about the whys and wherefores of that rash decision.

Instead he turned his head away to carry on exploring the shadowy spaces around them with his senses at full alert. Maybe if she had turned to crime to help her brother mend their fortunes she would be able to creep about in the dark as if it was her natural habitat as well. Still, it felt like a convenient way to shut her curiosity out so she tried to do the same to him, but only sniffed out a faint air of reverence and moss and old stone.

The remains of a few hundred years of prayer and observance were overlaid with the scent of sheep, she decided, as she tried to ape her husband's sharp sense of the world around them. Best beware where she sat, then, unless she wanted to smell of sheep droppings all the way to their destination.

In the end, she decided she didn't care if Will realised she didn't want to be alone when she followed him out to fetch her pony inside for the night as well. She tried to shrug off the odd feeling of loneliness in the company of the one man she had loved and longed for from the first moment she laid eyes on him.

At last the horses were both rubbed down and left with nosebags of oats to munch on and keep them quiet and she and Will sat down with their backs to a nearly intact wall. He passed her a chunk of still blessedly fresh bread and a hunk of cheese from his saddle bags and she ate hungrily, then grimaced at the taste of the beer in the flask he passed her, but she knew they were in sheep country so it probably wasn't safe to drink from the spring she could hear nearby.

Satisfied, if not exactly replete, she snuggled into her rough coat and decided she might as well try to sleep for an hour or two in their stony refuge with her man of stone so close she had only to reach out and touch him, but dared not for all the reasons she had already forced on her still barely suppressed passion for the wretched man.

'Oh, come here,' he whispered huskily as she shifted and fidgeted between the cold stone and close-cropped turf, trying to find a hollow she might be able to curl up into. 'You'll do yourself a mischief.'

'I can't lie in your arms like a block, Will,' she admitted unevenly.

If she snuggled close to him for warmth and comfort, it would be impossible to ignore the steady beat of his heart or the unique scent of him. Lying so close to him, feeling the wonder of him so real and alive when she butted up against him or snuggled into his arms for warmth in the night? No, the temptation would be too much. She would humiliate herself and beg and he might give in. While he might make love in silence, she knew she could not, not when self-control was the last thing on her mind when they were so intimate together she hardly knew where she ended and he began for the breathless wonder of it.

'You feel more like an ice block at the moment,' he said gruffly, then curled his big body around hers despite her resistance.

That resolution not to disgrace herself in his arms seeped out of her as she was warmed and soothed by his closeness and the grass under her body suddenly seemed springy and almost comfortable. Her pride was too fierce to let her admit how stiff and sore riding so far today had left her, but she still felt the tension and wariness of the day drain away because when Will was close, nothing else mattered to her but him.

He gently stroked her back as he wrapped himself even closer around her, like a big cat guarding his mate. She might as well close her eyes and enjoy it, she decided sleepily and nestled her head into the strong curve between his shoulder and neck with a blissful sigh. Everything she had ever wanted in life was here. Never mind they didn't even have a roof over their heads or a fire to keep the darkness at bay. His strong heart was beating steadily under her splayed hand, his breath was warm and even against her ear and she thought she felt him kiss the top of her head before he muttered very softly in that ear, 'Go to sleep, love.'

For once she did as she was told and let her doubts and fears and questions slip away because he was here and she loved him.

Chapter Fourteen

'We don't have time to sit and stare,' Will said when he turned around to find out why Helena had halted her pony to take a proper look down the wooded valley.

'I won't be cheated out of my first proper look at your home, Will,' she said fiercely. 'I refuse to let either of us be robbed of more than we have already lost.'

He rode back to her and persuaded his stubborn horse to stand the other way so he could watch her back while she gazed at the ancient stone roofs and many quirks of his late great-grandmother's beloved home.

'I have barely spent more than a few nights here since I grew up,' he argued gruffly as he scanned the forest rather than look at the rambling old manor house attached to the ruins of an ancient keep by one sturdy wall. 'My great-grandmother's will denied me full control of it until I was five and twenty, so of course I was too stubborn to come here for more than a day or so to make sure it was still standing before that day. I was too busy marrying you last time I was home properly to spare it even that long and I wanted it to be fully mine when I brought you here, you see? That's the sort of stubborn young idiot I was back then.'

'My idiot,' she said with a quick smile and gazed down at his home again. 'Was the castle built by the English or the Welsh?'

She knew he wanted to march her down to apparent safety at the double and never mind who built this quirky, lovely old home. There was no sense of warning in the air for her, nothing but the hopes and dreams fizzing inside her as she took in the peaceful seclusion of this heavily wooded valley and knew Will could find peace here, if only this threat he had felt hanging over him for so long was removed. The house below them and the whole dreamy feel of the place made it seem as if it had been waiting for him to come home for too long as well and here he was at last.

'Welsh,' he said shortly, then must have heard the ungraciousness of it, or maybe his great-grandmother's ghost was scolding him for such shocking manners. 'There is a legend of a Welsh princess hiding here from a rapacious Norman baron and transforming herself into an eagle so she could fly away when he tracked her down and battered her poor fortress into ruins.'

'Was that one of the stories your great-grandmother told you, or did you learn it when you were old enough to come here on your own after she died?'

He looked like a schoolboy caught out in a lie, but he was entitled to live here, to love this place as fiercely as her brother did his own wide acres and grand neo-classical mansion. 'I wasn't born a Welshman; I don't really feel I have a right to call this place home,' he said, finally turning around to face the same way as she was to look down on all he'd inherited, but could not live in since as a boy he had to go wherever his absent parents sent him and that was to Deepdale.

She supposed by the time he was old enough to choose for himself he was already in the

Army and too busy to come here for more than an odd, snatched week between deployments.

'Your great-grandmother must have thought you did or she would never have left it to you,' she pointed out.

'She was the last of her line.'

'No, you are that and I expect she could have found someone born and raised here if she wanted, but you are the one she loved so she left it to you instead.'

'What a poor and weary line to be forced to rely on me,' he said with a shrug and another impatient glance behind them. She heard his faint sigh and knew he must be thinking the earldom of Flamington would fall on his shoulders if he managed to outlive his uncle.

'Then it's our job to make that line stronger,' she said with a challenge to argue they would have no chance to make heirs for this lovely place and his uncle if his enemy had anything to do with it.

'I can't think of anything I would like better,' he said huskily and looked away from her again as if the idea was so impossible he dared not let himself believe in it. Her hatred for his cold-hearted and manipulative spymaster set hard even as she fought back tears because Will was still so wound up in fear for her he could not see the promise of this place and the family they could make together.

'Then believe in it, believe in us,' she challenged him and be damned to Will thinking he had to guard her back against a foe she was more and more convinced was too busy pretending Will's terrible dilemma had nothing to do with him to bother sneaking up on such a sharply aware former agent.

'I can but try,' he said hoarsely and there went another of his stern defences against her.

'Then forget your demon for a moment, Will. Sit here beside me and just see the promise of our future in front of us,' she urged and for a long, tense moment she thought he would ignore her and keep one eye on the steep slope behind them and only half his attention on the prospect ahead.

'Very well,' he said at last and she could feel him forcing his attention on to his fine old house, trying to open himself up to that future as well. His horse shifted and seemed to think about having a sly nip at her placid pony, but in the end even he stilled as well.

Helena saw Will's braced shoulders relax at last and such longing—so much pride in all this mellow, quirky beauty—as his careful guard dropped and he gave way to his emotions in broad daylight. And of course his guard on them had to be fearsome because he had so many of them to hide. He was complex and damaged and life with him was going to be the devil of a challenge but it was her challenge; her stubborn, gallant, over-protective lover and she would probably not have fallen in love with him in the first place if he was any less than all of that.

'I would go through everything again to have you beside me here now, Will, on your bad-tempered horse, looking forward to all the chaos and glory of raising our family here one day, God willing. I would willingly endure the hell of missing you without a hope of ever seeing you again twice over if it was the price I had to pay to sit here, knowing you are truly here and want a future with me nearly as much as I want one with you.'

'I do want it,' he said tersely, and she could see the longing in his darkest velvet brown eyes even if his doubts they would ever at-tain it stopped him meeting her gaze full on. 'I want it, but we can't have it until we are free of this devil, Helena.'

'I dare to believe it is going to happen, Will, even if you cannot quite manage to.'

'I want to, but dreams like that just make me more afraid. I could not live it without you and the serpent on my tail wants me to suffer so what better way to make sure I do than come after you?'

'We must live each moment we do have as if it's precious, then,' she told him crossly and dug her heels into the wide flanks of her pony to urge it towards what she hoped was a nice comfortable stable, a well-deserved rest and plenty to eat.

Following her like an obedient knight behind his queen, Will fumed silently as he kept his bigger and slightly faster mount to the pace of the smaller one she was on.

Live each moment...as if it's precious, indeed. What did she think he had been doing ever since he set eyes on her again?

He fought the roar of his own hot and seemingly endless need of her and the way she had always been able to stir his temper and make him feel things he wasn't sure he wanted to. She was right though, wasn't she? He did live as if every moment might be his or—worse—her last. He was so used to dreading his most precious secret being found out he had forgotten how to embrace simple joys or to feel so glad to see this place again and know the late summer heat was nestling into every challenging crevice of this beautiful land to at least try to gentle it for the storms to come.

He shivered at the memory of the bitter chill that iced him to his bones on the day he read his uncle's letter telling him that his mother had been murdered. Never mind heat and a very different country, he knew then the torture his enemy promised to inflict on him was only just beginning. Helena's life felt utterly precious as fear chilled him to his soul. So, he had to allow that murderous cur to make him a rat who lurked in places nobody else wanted to go.

In order to stop his enemy finding out he was married and leaving Will dead inside by killing his wife, Helena had to be his widow in silence for five long years. She had had to live with that heavy secret and *he* had burdened her with it like the thoughtless fool he was back then.

All because he was too proud to take his wife to war with him. It was never truly about danger or refusing to watch her going cold and hungry, or hot or bone weary. He was too proud to see his wife living less than comfortably. Lady Helena Snowe must stay clean and lovely, must keep her place as an aristocratic society beauty until he came home again. Then he would claim her as a returning hero and her family's opposition would melt away.

They could have been together every day and night since they were married if he had only seen how rare and precious love was. If he had only taken a good long look at his motives for leaving her behind, how different their lives could have been and now she was right again.

'Easy for you to say,' he muttered all the same.

No point letting her know she had lit a fire with her *live each moment we do have as if it's precious, then,* until they had the chance to do something about it.

She had braced her shoulders against him

and did not even turn around in the saddle to challenge him again. It wasn't going to be easy for him to change, he decided, but there had to be a better way of diverting her from dashing in where angels feared to tread than making her think she was rebuilding their marriage alone.

'All right, then, I will try harder,' he said a little louder. He tried not to sound defensive, but failed from the look of her stiffly held back. When she chose to use it, his wife had a gift for stony silence a Trappist monk would envy. They reached the path down through to the stables at last and she didn't ask him another question or look for any signs of life so he knew he was in deep trouble.

A boy rushed out of the walled garden before Will had to admit he was a coward again. The lad stopped so suddenly he nearly tumbled over his own feet, then gazed at them for a long moment before muttering something incomprehensible and running away. Will shrugged and hoped someone could speak English here. He cursed himself again for never having made the effort to learn the Welsh language.

'Lost then, are you?' a man's voice asked genially from behind them.

Will turned in his saddle to meet a pair of shrewd blue eyes that made him wonder if this man was the boy's father. 'No. Found, perhaps, but certainly not lost, Owain,' he said with a wry smile.

'Duw,' the man said after a second look. He paled and wiped a slightly grubby hand over his brow as if his eyes and ears could still be deceiving him. 'Master Will,' he said at last and shook his head in wonder and bafflement. 'They told us you were dead.'

'They told me I was as well,' he said with a sidelong glance at the magnificent but still-fuming woman at his side. If he worked really hard for the next fifty years, he might even deserve such a wife. 'You used to escort my great-grandmother to Deepdale when I was a boy. My uncle told me he had appointed you as land agent here.'

'Aye, well, fancy you remembering me after all these years.'

The man still looked shocked Will was alive and he wondered what that could mean to people he had neglected as an absentee landlord. He clearly had another lot of hard work to do if he was going to convince them it was a change for the better.

'I might have been a heedless young lad at the time, but I still took more notice than I pretended.'

'Well now, I'm that glad you're alive after all, sir. We hardly knew what to do for the best without anyone to sort things out here.'

'I will do my best to make up for lost time now I am here,' he said, 'but in the meantime, my wife is in need of a hot bath and a change of clothing; any sort of clothing would probably feel better than what she is wearing now,' he added with a wary look at her to admit he'd inflicted those shabby rags on her and felt truly ashamed. Although they had concealed some of her delicious feminine curves from the hungry eyes of the world...and her husband.

'A clean flour sack would feel better than the things I have on,' Helena said with a shrug and a rueful smile for Owain that Will envied him.

He was still in deep trouble with her, then. Fair enough, but a man could only be penitent for so long, especially after being ordered to become a better husband forthwith. He glanced at her again and, heavens, how he wanted her. He forgot to be on edge and weary of running away because even dressed like that she was so deliciously desirable he felt dangerous.

Even when she was refusing to be flustered about being seen by his estate manager in her boy's raiment, on a hill pony, with a day and a half of wind and sun and dirt on her haughty countenance, she was stormily unique and utterly desirable. Best not look at her any more or they wouldn't even be able to make it to the house before he fell on her like a hungry bear.

'A flour sack, is it?' Owain said, 'I'm sure that can be arranged, milady.'

Will wondered how he knew about her title, but of course he didn't, it was her regal bearing and refusal to admit there was anything out of the ordinary about her scruffy boy's raiment that gave Her Highness away.

'She really is a milady as it happens, Owain. Lady Helena Harborough, may I present Owain ap Huw, my estate manager?'

'Good day to you, Mr ap Huw,' she said with a cool look at Will as if even her title was his fault at the moment.

'I'll go and see about that bath, then, my lady.'

'Owain, our arrival must remain a secret for the time being,' Will cautioned before he could do that and the gossip began to fly around the area like wildfire.

'Ah, I suppose that accounts for the breech...' Owain let his voice tail off as he realised where his tongue was about to go. He turned away before it went anywhere else and Will heard him calling the boy and cautioning him to keep silent with fatherly affection.

Stupid to suddenly feel the warmth of unshed tears at the back of his eyes because the child he and Helena had married to protect had never happened. If he wasn't a fool, they could have had a child by now—maybe even two or three of them. He wondered if Helena had the same regrets he had had to learn to live with about their lost potential sons and daughters.

Now he had let himself feel again he longed to watch her grow big with their child. He wanted it so badly he had a rigid arousal to fight now and thinking of all the fun they could have begetting one was not helping him control it.

'About that flour sack...' he said, the very idea of her wearing one as a makeshift chemise prompting a wolfish grin.

'If you think you're coming anywhere near me until I feel like a proper woman again, then think again, Major Harborough.'

'You are always a proper woman to me, although I can always hope for a bit of improperness now and again,' he said with a pretend leer and knew she was trying not to laugh even if she was doing her best to pretend otherwise.

'Go away and leave me alone,' she ordered him crisply.

'For now,' he said and made himself let go of the fantasy he could join her in her bath, soap her satin skin until the grass stains and good Welsh dirt and even the faint whiff of sheep was quite gone. Then they could make love on the bed conveniently waiting for them in his eager fantasy. Anyway, before he could have the dream, he had to be sure they were both alive to dream it.

Chapter Fifteen

It had taken an hour for enough water to heat for her bath and another to get herself thoroughly clean and dressed in the oddest collection of finery she ever did see. Now Helena was sitting in the hastily swept and dusted parlour, waiting for Will to return. He was sure to have been busy making this place as secure as he could without alerting the entire area to their presence and he had needed a bath and shave as well, so goodness knew when she was going to see him again.

She sighed and suspected he would try to keep her here where she would be watched over even if she did manage to drive the spectre of this phantom avenger out of his stubborn head. He had this estate to put in order however well Owain had looked after it while he was gone, then there were Lord Flamington's vast acres to help Will's uncle run in Wiltshire.

Will's peculiar upbringing, despite his doting Welsh great-grandmother and the Spanish grandmother he spoke of with exasperated fondness, meant he could never have felt he truly belonged anywhere and she fiercely wanted him to feel he did now. This place was old fashioned and had not been lived in for too long, but it was still a home, not a stately mansion. It felt like the place both of them needed before the huge responsibility of Deepdale descended on them one day.

The trouble with falling head over ears in love with a serving soldier was you had no time to know each other properly before you married. She had been so afraid she would lose him she had wanted them to love completely before he had to go back to his duties. A whisper of guilt had always haunted her because she had schemed so hard to get him to the altar and it slipped back in now and undermined her confidence in their love match all these years later.

She had done everything she could to undermine his steely willpower until she finally got him into that dark room and exploded a whole magazine of gunpowder under it, but even now she wasn't truly sorry. Yet because of her impatience someone was able to push Will further than any man ought to have to go and now they would have to learn one another almost from scratch. Right now it felt like playing chess without knowing the rules, but she was determined to learn them somehow.

First, she would have to forgive him for protecting her so fiercely from the chaos and carnage of his life as a soldier. But how would she convince him he could not remove every hazard in her path? All women faced obstacles a man never would so she had never been able to work out why they were supposed to be the weaker sex.

She had to believe she would survive childbirth if she conceived his child and she wanted one so badly it looked like a risk worth taking. She wanted a pack of wilful and contrary little beings if only they could have them. She could hardly wait to find out if they followed Will's dark good looks or the fairer, slighter

Snowes and she hugged her arms across her slender waist, getting lost in a fantasy that it might soon disappear under an ever-expanding baby bump.

'That's a very serious expression,' Will said from the doorway.

'I was wondering how long it would take to turn this place into a home again,' she lied.

'Maybe we could start by just living in it and go from there,' he said practically.

'You sound like Captain Harborough eyeing up his latest billet,' she replied and saw his smile fade. 'I doubt Major Harborough needed to worry about billets for his men or keeping them fed since you were too busy being a lone wolf to have any by then,' she tried to joke, but only made it feel worse. 'Shall we always have to tiptoe around each other's sore spots like this, Will?' she asked with a sigh because she felt so clumsy and careless for stamping on one or two of his without meaning to.

'No! I'll be damned if we will,' he said and came properly into the room to stare down at her with so much more of her darling Will in his eyes than she dared hope for even yesterday. 'My enemy has robbed us of enough already.'

'True,' she murmured, wondering how he would feel when he found out she believed in that enemy less with every mile they had travelled here, but decided there was no point worrying about it until his supposed friend turned up to confirm or deny her suspicions. 'We have such a lot of lost time to make up, although I fear our bedchamber is currently being spring cleaned in a great flurry of dust and polishing and airing out that looked as if it might take the rest of the day,' she said wistfully.

'Marriage isn't only about bed, my Helena,' he said mock sternly.

'True, but mine has felt so empty for so long I refuse to pretend I don't yearn to be in one with you quite shamelessly now you have come back to life and if that makes me wanton, I don't care.'

'Nor do I and it makes you frank and delicious and only wanton with me,' he told her, though he still firmed his jaw and watched her as if he was trying his hardest to remind himself they had a great deal to do here besides make love and, hopefully, babies.

'When I am with you my rational mind slips off into the woods and hides and the rest of me just needs and wants you. All those years of bitter frustration seem to have built so much longing inside me I feel as if I have to keep proving we are real,' she admitted quietly.

His eyes went velvet dark at the thought of all the frustration she had wrestled with for so long and he let his own show as if he had finally given himself permission to be ravenous as well. She didn't think either of them could wait until tonight. No, that was wrong; she *knew* she could not and hoped he could not either.

'Ah, my Helena,' he said gruffly and held out his hand in a yearning gesture that gave lie to any rational decision he might have made to wait to make love like cool and civilised beings.

'Ah, my Will,' she echoed almost mockingly, but with such a warm, wicked, encouraging smile he pulled her out of her chair and into his arms and thank goodness for that. 'I have missed you so much,' she murmured, meaning since their first frantic lovemaking two whole nights ago, but if he took it as six and a half years' worth of missing him, that was all well and good.

'I was so sure I must not admit to it until I finally got my enemy off our tails, but I love you, Helena,' he said on a stuttering sigh that almost made her forget he had been trying to hold her at a distance since their last loving in the rosy dawn.

'What else *but* love made you hide yourself for so long, Will? What else could be big enough to make you lie that you were dead for so long, you great fool?' she whispered with tears in her eyes as she hit his shoulder with half-hearted force to say he was just plain daft to think it could be anything less. She had promised herself she would not cry again, but she could not hold the tears back now.

'Guilty as changed, milady,' he told her with a wry look and he kissed first one eyelid, then the other and the gentle brush of his mouth against her eyelashes felt so intriguing and intimate she managed to stop crying after all. If all her tears had ended like these how rich her life would have been so far.

'I admit to being a fool this once, my clever love,' he whispered. 'I was certainly a fool to think I could stop loving you while there is a breath in my body. I had such nightmares of you meeting another man when you thought I was dead, I should have known it was always love,' he said ruefully.

Despite trying to make light of those nightmares she felt a shudder go through his whipcord-strong body and she realised he had lived through almost as much heartache during those aching, empty years apart as she had, even if he had at least known she was alive to yearn for when he let himself.

'I could never love another man as I do you, my darling,' she murmured and brushed a sneaky kiss across one of his prominent cheekbones, then stood face to face with him. Suddenly she realised he was too thin as well; what a fine one he was to talk about her weight loss while they were apart. 'I could never love again if it comes to that,' she added in case he had any doubts left. 'What would be the point in trying to when I know real love should feel like you do?'

'Nobody could love me like you do,' he told

her unsteadily, then shook his head as if he knew he didn't have the right words to tell her the truth in his dear, darkest of brown eyes. 'You had every right to love someone else less than me, while I was away, Helena. I am lucky you were tied to Hawley being your brother's right-hand woman for most of the time I was gone. If some other rogue had seen you, he might have spent the last five years persuading you otherwise.'

'Nobody ever will, Rake Harborough,' she said, standing on tiptoe to murmur it in his ear and remind him how she loved the rogue he was when he was still pretending to be one.

'Not even respectable Mr Harborough? He *will* be disappointed.'

'No, he won't,' she argued huskily and wriggled closer to the insistent evidence both the rake and the respectable man of property wanted her very urgently and preferably right now. 'One thing I can promise is a lack of that kind of disappointment in Mr Harborough's immediate future. Providing he overcomes his diffidence about shocking his servants and I really hope he is going to do that because

I need him so much,' she added throatily. 'I need you so much it hurts.'

'And we can't have that, now, can we?' he said unsteadily. A faint thump in the distance made him tense against the prospect of them being caught in the act by their servants, or an over-eager visitor who might have chanced on a secret to set the whole neighbourhood by the ears. 'Upstairs,' he whispered tersely.

'Hurry, then,' she whispered, because she was about to stop caring who caught them making love on the nearest convenient surface as long as they made it straight away.

In the end they found a lovely old room on the next floor up from the cleaning and rear-ranging and shut the door on the world. Will removed the odd assortment of dated outer garments Helena was wearing, then paused. 'I would almost have preferred the flour sack,' he told her as her bodice flew across the room and he gazed down at her as she sank back on to the bed in a nip-waisted corset and padded silk underskirt designed to bell out over pan-niers when it was made who knew how many years ago. 'My great-grandmother must have worn this at Court in the Dark Ages.'

'Apparently, she refused to change her mode of dress after your great-grandfather died so there was nothing else to wear but the rags I came in since Owain's wife is half a foot smaller than me. Do I look like a quiz?'

'You look delicious,' he said unsteadily. 'But the flour sack would have been so much easier to get off,' he added with a frown at the pale blue damask stays that gave her breasts rather more fullness than nature intended, but laced up the back so once she was in them, she needed assistance to get out again.

'Now I rather like it,' she told him with a provocative look down at her more lush than usual bosom, then she laughed huskily at the frustration in his dark eyes as he brooded on how to get his hands on her breasts and, hopefully, his mouth as well, and sooner rather than later.

'Let me up again, then, so you can undo the knot at the back for me,' she told him and knelt upright so he could reach around her back to fumble with that knot, to their mutual frustration. 'Concentrate,' she ordered as he took the chance to whisper teasing kisses around the low back of the corset as he turned her round so he could see what he was doing. His deliberately light touch made her shiver with frustrated anticipation of his lust-driven fingers on her bare skin.

'Impossible,' he whispered, then pushed her mass of tumbling curls aside and forgot why he was round there as he worked his way up her backbone with provocative licks and kisses, then praised the vulnerable curve of her exposed neck until she was shaking with need.

'Hurry,' she gasped out as heady desire shot through her like a wildfire, but he seemed to have changed his mind about being hot and hasty and ignored her wriggling and trying to skew around to get at him. Instead of allowing her to lay her impatient hands on his hard, aroused body, he held her gently but firmly by her waist and went on with his tortuous, sensual, patient exploration of the exposed parts of her back above the stays that nipped her in and pushed her into a shape she didn't know she could go into until she wore them.

'No, this time is for you,' he argued with a

rasp in his voice that was some comfort because it let her know it was costing him all the willpower he had to keep still and so ridiculously, arousingly patient behind her as he caressed her. He held on to this determination not to do as she urged and hurry until they were both at the far edges of their sanity and beyond all restraint. 'Remember how you always loved being petted and praised when we loved before?'

She could not speak for wanting more and only nodded as the memory of him learning her inch by inch on their honeymoon made her shiver under his exploring touch and long even more for the completion he was holding back from them. She wanted culmination and satisfaction. He could explore her at their leisure afterwards and then they could do it all again.

'Want,' she managed to gasp through kiss-hungry lips and wished there was a mirror handy so she could see how he looked as well, know whether he was desperate enough for a wriggle or a keen in the right direction to unman him and get her what she wanted instead of when he thought she wanted. She was beyond ready and on the brink of catching fire all on her own again.

'For now want must be your master, then, my Lady Helena Snowe,' he told her with the wickedly sensual whisper of his index finger running down her spine and following the curves of the wretched, embracing, exposing corset. A long, delicious shiver shook every aroused and sensitised inch of her from head to toe.

'Enela ha' bro,' was the only incoherent protest she could manage to push out of her hungry mouth as more delicious shivers racked through her and he threaded wicked kisses around the base of her neck and kept his grip on her waist to resist the wriggle she so badly wanted to make against his manhood to say stop teasing and just do, for goodness sake.

'Keep still and behave yourself, madam. I mean to praise and pet you and drive you wild with untamed desire over and over again, my very particular Lady Helena Harborough,' he told her and she realised he intended to be fully in command of this lovemaking for all she had managed to ride roughshod over him last time because it was such a wickedly, painfully long time since they had had one another in a bed together and a whole night ahead of them for the ultimate in pleasure.

Somehow control between them had slipped out of her hands this time, but with his mouth warm on the side of her throat now and the feel of his powerful body tense behind her she could not bring herself to care which of them was in command as long as they got where they needed to be before she burst into flames.

Every kiss and lick and caress sent more of her beyond where they had been before and made her wonder how much control they still had left between them. Too much, she decided as his stern but never hurting hands on her waist only hinted at his state of arousal and his ability to fight it for her increased pleasure felt almost too much. It certainly felt more urgent for her to feel his hands deliciously exploring her body to the very edge of reason when he knelt behind her to caress her needy breasts.

She could actually hear the abrasion of his calloused hands on the rich silk of her corset as well as feel the warm reality of them a whisper away from her eager nipples. He gave a grunt of masculine appreciation as he felt them harden even more under his exploring fingers. She heard herself moan half in satisfaction and half in protest that this was all the contact he was allowing them.

She knew he was watching over her shoulder as her breasts peaked and rose with the force of her desire and fought against the restraint of the stays . If she had enough wits left to speak, she could purr as she imagined the sensual appreciation of the velvet dark depths his wonderful eyes as they lingered on the welcome she wanted to gift him so badly, but he still managed to hold her just far enough away for her to feel her own shattering arousal and not his.

'Will…oh, my Will,' she managed to mutter between bitten lips numb and awed with wanting everything he had to give her.

She wanted his kisses wherever she could get them. She needed his deep caresses on those needy nipples so hard and burning against their imprisonment. She wanted him to give up this sweet torture and plunge into her hot, slick welcome until they were both incoherent with urgency and halfway to the stars from the very moment he thrust hard and rigidly aroused inside her and want caught up with him at long last.

At the same time she wanted him to hold her suspended between luxurious satisfaction and glorious anticipation for as long as human willpower could keep them here. Except his seemed so much stronger than hers she had to trust him to know how long that was possible before they melted independently of one another and a spectacular mutual climax was lost to them until next time.

'Helena,' was all he said, but the infinite satisfaction of having her hungry breasts and outrageously wanting him nipples under his hands again was enough to tell her so much more than his rusty-sounding voice.

Moving a little further on to the bed behind her, he stroked and flattered those breasts until they rose even more impudently above the stiffly silky stuff as she looked down at them cupped by his tanned and, oh, so delightfully flexible hands. They looked rich and creamy and unusually full against the contrast of pale blue damask and her very alive and wanting her husband's sensual touch.

She felt so feminine and powerful and

needy she was beyond words and keened her need for more and didn't even have a scruple to spare for any of their people who might realise what the master and mistress of the house were up to from the sound of her sensuous whimpers for more in this wrapped-up bedchamber high up in the eaves. She almost smiled as she heard herself sound like a hungry kitten in need of every comfort it had been deprived of and then a lot like a throaty mama cat calling for her mate to make one in the first place.

Feeling Will slide one hand under the tight prison of her silken stays, she let her head fall back against his shoulder and gasped out a demand for more and a far more urgent touch. He caressed and explored and whispered praise in her ear, then stopped to kiss it and praise that in its turn, and she finally managed to push back against his body and feel the rampant pressure of his desire for her against her backside, then do it again with a long moan of frustrated pleasure.

'Soon,' he whispered and seemed to call up another iota of control to draw a little back from her and rearrange them so she was almost overflowing her damask stays as her weight was thrust further forward and he cursed the ties of her elaborate petticoat. 'That can stay,' he told her with another appreciative stroke of the rich material of her outrageously low-cut stays, 'but this has to go,' he added and finally got the ties around her waist undone.

'Lift up,' he ordered and she did as he bid and hoped he didn't think this much wifely obedience was habit forming, although if this was the result, perhaps she could endure being an obedient wife every now and again in secret. 'That's it,' he told her with extreme satisfaction as the clumsy padded petticoat slipped off at last, but how the devil did the man still have words when she certainly wasn't wearing any drawers to cover up her extreme desire.

He must be able to scent and see the warmth of the welcome she had waiting for him as she sank her knees back on to the soft feather mattress with a frustrated gasp. She was beyond words so she did the only thing she could to hasten the joining she was beyond desperate for now. She rotated her hips and felt the delicious abrasion of his manhood through his still confoundedly done-up breeches and he groaned with need behind her.

'Off,' she demanded and felt him check and seem shocked, as if he believed he meant get off her. 'Them off you,' she managed to string enough words together to let him know she was impatient for all of him, not in the midst of changing her mind for some inexplicable reason; as if she could even think of doing that when she felt as if she would break if he didn't complete them very soon.

'Stay just where you are then,' he said as if she was a sculptor's model whom he wanted to hold her outrageous pose for posterity to marvel at.

She almost had the giggles at the thought of such a scandalous image preserved for as long as marble or bronze lasted, but she was too interested in the sound of the clunk of his boots hitting the floor and the hasty unbuttoning and undoing he was evidently scurrying through to take in what an outrageous idea it was.

Then he was back and oh, bliss, he was caressing her waist again, but with more serious intent. He drew her closer to what she hoped was the consummation she had longed for ever since the last one ended. He had aroused every sense she had to the very zenith of anticipation and she had done as he ordered and stayed here like a very indecent statue waiting for her lord and master to take her.

He repaid her by caressing and kissing the line at the base of this ancient old piece of temptation of the corsetière's art instead of the top. She felt his lips on the dip of her spine just before it blossomed into the honed curves of her bottom and gasped anew with sensations she had never even dreamed could feel so delicious there until today.

Even as she was open mouthed with awe at his amorous expertise, he took her nether cheeks in his hands and caressed them firmly apart and the warmth of her welcome seemed to break his tethers at long last because he gave a long, guttural gasp and entered her in one glorious, generous thrust until he was inside her as high as he could go and as hard as velvet-wrapped steel.

She felt him pause as if he was trying to gentle himself, grab the reins back and give her everything she wanted instead of the driven taking she sensed him struggling to hold back for her benefit. She wouldn't have minded it after that tortuous, praising, edgy build up, but he still exerted his mighty will-power and managed to tame that fiery demand they gallop for the finish line to give her every ounce of pleasure they had in them.

He caressed the tender skin of her neck with his tongue, mouthed hot praise against her willing ears as he bent over her to thrust harder and faster and whisper wondrous things as he used their novel position to find the sweetest spot he could and abrade it with his very aroused manhood. She began to convulse around him and couldn't hold on to her drive to absolute pleasure a moment longer since she was almost there.

At last his rhythm went deeper and stronger as he felt her convulse in the wildest extreme of pleasure she had ever experienced and she went boneless, then convulsed again all the way up to the music of the spheres and met him there. It felt as if their very souls were locked in a dance as sweet as life itself and way beyond time's busy ticking. Here was absolute intimacy, complete trust and they were together inside it. It felt utterly delicious and there were simply no words for how glorious it felt to soar in his arms, to convulse and bow together in such extreme ecstasy her senses nearly left her for it.

One last great, wrenching thrust and she felt his seed pour into her and dearly hoped that could mean they had begun a child. Even if they had not, pleasure like this was a wondrous gift to be treasured. As she felt him drive one last long, delicious thrust into her aching-with-pleasure core, she knew they had everything they could ever need together and wasn't their life wonderful?

'Oh, my love,' she murmured as they drifted back to some thready kind of sanity on the other side of such pleasure it went beyond even her wildest dreams until today. She pushed back against him one last time as he went to withdraw so he could set her the right way up and she could gaze at her lover with dazed wonder they still had so much to learn about pleasuring one another. 'My love,' she repeated as she felt him stir inside her then withdraw anyway, as if he was shocked by his rampant need of his temporarily sated wife.

'As if I can ever have enough of you after what we have been through,' she whispered as they finally turned to one another and she watched him try to reassemble some defence against her and fail. His feelings shone in his dark and complicated gaze as he faced her without any of the barriers he had held against the world at last. Here he was, her young, endlessly ardent lover—her one and only love. Now he was Major Harborough as well, the man who had given all he was to protect her, the great, grand, gallant fool.

He frowned and stayed silent and brooding for a long moment as she felt a prickle of worry slide under her absolute joy in what they had just done together. Then she saw a glint of tears in his velvet brown eyes and knew he was fighting them too hard to say how he felt. He would think it was so unmanly to shed even one in front of her and she smiled at him with such tenderness she almost cried as well. Instead she smoothed one of his frowning dark brows and those bitter, reluctant tears spilled on to her loving fingertip.

'It's all right, my love. It's allowed,' she crooned in his ear and pushed him down on to the bed so she could crawl into his side and warm him with every bit of her she could squirm against his now shivering body. 'With me, everything is allowed,' she whispered and stroked the hand he raised to hide his eyes, as if even she should not know he was undone by loving her.

Her fury at the manipulation that made her sensitive, proud, striving love so wound up in its toils it took the end of a war to free him felt fierce inside her. A weapon she fully intended to use against whoever really dared wound him so deeply. She stroked Will's silver-dusted dark curls and silently swore to do everything she could to be sure he acquired no more grey hairs until he had a right to them.

After another twenty years or so as her rampant, much-loved husband—and, hopefully, the father of a vast brood—he might be allowed to add one or two more. Before then he would have all the good things in life denied him for so long, even if she had to expose his so-called friend's misuse of Will's loving heart and tender conscience for all the world to see.

'I could not allow myself to think about

you lest I ran mad from missing you, wanting you, needing you,' he finally muttered into her ear as she snuggled into his shoulder and hugged him so close the corset irked her with its bones, but its ancient seduction had still been worth it so she abraded the rich brocade against his gloriously powerful torso and felt every muscle in him tighten without any permission from his conscious mind.

'I had to empty myself out to do what I did, Helena. I needed to pretend I was stone and ice to guard you from him. I hated what I did, but I had to do it,' he told her bleakly, as if he ought to be ashamed of himself for feeling so much instead of the little he had pretended for so long. 'All those years I didn't deserve to love you, my darling, I didn't deserve to live,' he ended and she felt the warmth and wetness of his tears against her bare skin and wriggled even closer to him.

'You did deserve it and everything we managed to have together and be together. You deserve it even more because of what you had to do to yourself to keep faith with what we promised one another years ago,' she argued, but felt him shake his head and fight not to be comforted. She heard his silent argument and shook her head to tell him he was so wrong.

'You are not allowed to argue with me, Major. You owe me six and a half years of loving, for being without this, being without you. Just accept what I say for once in your stubborn life, you great idiot, and tremble because the price I intend to extract from you is a promise to love me immoderately for the rest of my life and be my darling Will again.

'I am ready to admit you were arrogant and far too sure of yourself in the old days, but you have the most generous heart I ever came across and you didn't even know it until I snatched it off you for safekeeping. In return I expect you to be my vigorous and dashingly handsome lover again instead of a poor, broken-down, grey-haired major.'

Had she gone too far? She felt him flinch when she ran a loving, slightly shaking hand over that dark hair of his, too grey for a man in his healthy and rampant prime. He seemed to want to resist the fact he was a young and very vigorous man. She held her breath while he fought with his demons before he at last relaxed and snuggled her even closer to his vigorous masculine body, as if he could never get enough of the feel of them as lovers again either.

Insatiable sensual curiosity stirred inside her yet again and she wanted more than his butterfly caress on her own now very tangled hair, but maybe this was something they had to resolve before they could love again. At last he raised his dear head and met her eyes without his usual wary defences.

'Harridan,' he told her in a husky whisper. 'You will probably be the death of me, my insatiable, demanding hussy,' he said and, even if his smile was wry and a little bit wobbly, the laughing devils she first fell in love with in Rake Harborough's darkest of brown eyes one fateful night in Mayfair were hotly alive again.

'But you'll die happy and take me with you,' she said smugly, and tugged impudently on his already aroused again sex. And that was the last thing either of them said for quite some time.

Chapter Sixteen

'We need to talk, Will,' Helena told her supposedly exhausted husband much later, even if she didn't want to bring the shadows of the past into this lovely old room and the looming problem of how to properly unravel it.

'Maybe we do,' he said, playing with a long strand of gold-flecked chestnut hair and arranging it over her shoulders as if the contrast of creamy white skin with the fiery dark mass of it fascinated him. 'You know how you wore your hair in a crop when we first met?' he said as he smoothed her long locks as if he loved them. 'It made you look like an eager, elfin princess, but now you are more like a queen,' he said as if he found that even more magnificent, but how could he when she was so much older, so much more worn down by life and missing him?

'I am eight and twenty years old now, Will. I had to change a lot of things while you were gone and it was cheaper to let it grow. We hardly had sixpence left to scratch with after Papa died,' she said with a quick twinge of regret. 'I am very far from regal, I am afraid.'

'Have you looked at yourself in the mirror lately, my lady?'

'I didn't dare after a very flustered maid and your friend's wife and the caretaker ran around the house trying to find whatever they could lay their hands on to make me decent again,' she joked, but there was a truth underneath it she didn't want to even think about. She had not spent much time looking in mirrors since he left her behind all those years ago. At first, she didn't want to meet the loneliness in her own eyes and then there wasn't time. Recently it was because she was too conscious life was passing her by. She had lost the softness of youth and privilege she had when they first met.

'Then allow me to introduce you,' he said and leapt out of bed to grab a looking glass from the nearest chest of drawers and wipe the dust off it with whatever came to hand before hurrying back to the bed, her hungry eyes intent on his fine and manly body, refusing to even think about whatever transformation he imagined she had miraculously pulled off since she last looked in one.

He caught her caressing, thoughtful gaze on his pared-down masculine body and one part of it in particular and shook his head chidingly before slipping back under the ancient bedcover so she could only see him from the waist up. That was temptation enough if he would not let her indulge in love games until she did what he wanted.

She stubbornly refused to turn her eyes away from him on to the mirror he was holding in front of her as if she ought to be proud to see herself as she was now and not how he must remember her, when she was all soft curves and youthful eagerness and so smooth skinned and silk clad she felt virulently jealous of her former self.

'Lady Helena Harborough, meet the Siren of Castle Eyrie. Siren of Mine, meet Lady Helena the Utterly Delicious and Desirable, wife of a very lucky fool who has never deserved her, but swears he will adore her as she deserves for the rest of their lives.'

'Idiot,' she told him with an almost playful smack on the hand holding the wretched thing up so close she would have to look or they would both know what a coward she was.

'Not at all, she's a witch and a wonder, my lady of slender patience and endless twists and turns.'

'Is she now?'

'Yes, she is and every one of them fascinates me. Just take a proper look at yourself for once, Helena. See? You are so beautiful. No, that's wrong...' She made a moue of disappointed protest as she finally did as he bid. If he was already taking it back, he must have seen the faint shadows under her eyes and the tautness of her skin over cheekbones where there was once soft youth and suppleness. He seemed to read her mind and shook his head. 'Not that sort of wrong, you nitwit. You are extraordinary, the one woman I—'

'I am not a nitwit,' she interrupted him crossly and the skinny female in the mirror looked even worse when she frowned. It seemed so unfair he looked even more manly and distinguished when age and grief had been so cruel to Lady Helena Snowe.

No, she was not Lady Helena Snowe, she had been lying about that for years—she was Lady Helena Harborough. She supposed as they truly did love one another she must take his word for it and if he saw her through the rosy haze of mutual desire she would merely thank her stars. 'And I am not beautiful now, if I ever was. I could never see it myself even when I was young.'

'You are terrible at seeing what is right in front of you, then, so let's get back to you learning to see yourself properly. Look how incredible your eyes look in that pared-down face you keep telling me is not as lovely as it used to be and you lie, by the way,' he said, running a long, caressing finger over her high cheekbones as she looked over the mirror to find his gaze and lose herself in it.

'No, you are to keep watching yourself until I convince you every finest fraction of you is wondrous to me,' he chided her and it felt so impossibly erotic to sit here naked while he brushed thistledown-soft caresses over her eager skin and she watched her own eyes go wider, her clear black pupils flaring and contracting with need while he watched her watching herself and realising how she looked flushed with wanting him so badly all over again and so soon as well.

He used that lazy finger to shape around her hairline and down, his touch worshipping as he outlined the stark oval of her face and she began to believe it really was beautiful to him as he drew in a stuttering breath and muttered, 'See? So beautiful.'

'So old, Will,' she whispered and those years apart threatened to slide back into the room and make her weep in her turn for all the waste and blankness of her time without him.

'Being stubborn as usual,' he chided, refusing to do as she longed for him to do and chase that searching, provoking finger over her lips...and he knew it, the great tease. Instead, he outlined her stubborn chin and chuckled as she set it even more defiantly to argue she wasn't stubborn at all, she was realistic and rational about her faded charms.

'Damnation take it, kiss me, you lout,' she ordered crossly, but instead he stopped her mouth with that exploring finger and shook his head at her as if he despaired of teaching such a reluctant pupil her lessons.

'Not until you admit you are as beautiful as you are instead of castigating yourself for being just a little younger than I am. You must love yourself if you are ever going to love me fully and I want that so much now you have got me started on loving again, my Helena. I want to know every last delicious inch of you and every stubborn thought in your contrary head.'

'You already have it all, you know that. You must have known it from the moment we first set eyes on one another.'

'Only because you had the self-confidence to know it was mutual in every way back then. If I had met you last week instead of six and a half years ago, would you believe love can be that instant and true for the lucky few we became a part of that night?'

The woman in the mirror frowned as his words hit home. 'I would have to because true love is so precious. It would be unthinkable to turn it aside and not hope against hope it was mutual,' she said at last. It was an admission she had to let him enjoy the delusions of a lover. Maybe they could only see the best in the beloved and he did not even care about the fine lines at the corner of her eyes or the changes five years of grieving made to her face and body.

'Then look past whatever faults you are eyeing up and see what I see; see the lovely truth of you, the faith you kept without hope, the grace and beauty and fineness that makes every other woman fade in comparison.'

'I am not that good or fine, Will, but you are right about me being stubborn and opinionated and I know I shall exasperate you until you want to throw things or gallop off your temper from here to Deepdale at times. I am no paragon; please say you didn't make me into one while you were pretending to be dead. I am so human it hurts and so headstrong I might have to ride away for both our sakes instead of you now and again.'

'You're clearly a harridan in the making,' he told her with so much love and laughter in his gaze her heart felt as if it really had turned over. 'I don't know how I can be mad enough to love and adore such a virago but, somehow,

I still do. What a fine dance we shall lead one another, my lovely,' he said and before he could recall the shadow over that dance, she pushed the hand still holding up that fine old mirror to the side and threw herself at him in a tangle of bedcovers and naked limbs.

They laughed even as she brought her face close to his and stared down at him with a vengeful gleam in her eyes. She soon forgot all about punishing him for that pretend volte face and they kissed and licked and whispered and moaned lovers' stuttering groans at one another, loving one another all over again. Tangled and captured and utterly, utterly contented their passion soared again and until at last they lay in one another's arms beyond words. Skin on skin, they slept away the afternoon.

By the end of the week Helena had managed to gather up a slender wardrobe of hastily sewn gowns that she and Owain's wife, Catrin, had to ransack the attics for. Ancient gowns had been cut up and remade in modern styles and they even found a bolt of unused cloth to make one up from scratch. Since

Will insisted she stay close to the house and they kept their presence here as secret as they could, the house was still far short of the polished perfection Catrin expected of this lovely old place now it finally had a master and a mistress again.

Helena rather liked it as it was, only half awake after its long sleep and so peaceful she could sit and dream of it coming fully alive with chatter and slightly scuffed by childish wear and tear as she and Will forged the life and home they both needed to make here. It felt right to get the true measure of this ancient house and its quirks and eccentric old ways before they set about making it fit their nineteenth-century lives a little better than it did now, all while somehow keeping its unique character.

'Busy, my love?' Will's deep voice said from the open doorway. It made her jump, but he seemed to have developed a habit of doing that lately, or perhaps she was simply dreaming more.

He claimed he enjoyed watching her when she was so lost in thought or lusty, longing fantasies of him that she forgot the rest of the world existed. Sometimes she would admit that was exactly what she was doing with a smile and sometimes she pretended she was thinking of laundry lists or how they were ever going to acquire all the things they needed when he was so reluctant to advertise their presence.

Either way, they usually ended up in their almost-grand-again bedchamber with the door shut behind them or went up to the dear old room up in the eaves where they had first made hasty love in their own home.

'Still trying to get myself decently clothed,' she told him ruefully and tried not to smile at the rakish grin he shot her so they both re-membered why that was such an uphill strug-gle for her.

'Maybe I prefer you indecently clothed,' he drawled and raised an eyebrow to say he was willing to revisit that delightful state of affairs.

'Not if the vicar calls or your staff find an-other crisis urgently in need of solving by the master of all he surveys,' she argued almost primly, despite the familiar breath-stealing de-sire that had eagerly stirred back into fiery life inside her at the mere sight of him, let alone the intimate promise of a lot more if she encouraged his husbandly attentions.

'Confound it, this time it sounds as if the vicar really might have arrived to find out if all those wild rumours are true and we are not just a pair of unlikely ghosts come to haunt him,' Will said with a frown and what looked like a tightening of every muscle at the sound of a new arrival to remind her he still thought they were in danger. Maybe she should feel guilty about secretly disagreeing him almost since the moment he'd told her about it and not saying so.

Owain's loud shout for the grooms to tend to the gentleman's horses until he was ready to leave again sounded like a warning that here was someone more dangerous than the local vicar outside. Helena's heart raced at the thought of a danger she had thought she was too angry to feel menaced by, but somehow she still managed it. If she was right about this particular arrival, Will might refuse to believe what she was sure his supposed friend and spymaster had done to him.

Fear that he would take the man's word over her reading of the tragic situation Will had been forced into by his friend slashed at the lovely confidence and the humour and mutual love she and Will had built together over the last delicious days of rediscovered passion. The love that had bound them together from the instant their wandering glances met across a crowded room all those years ago ought to be strong enough to weather this, even if she turned out to be wrong. Somehow, she did not think that she was and maybe he would find it unforgivable of her not to have warned him of what she had suspected all along.

She was so glad their absolute intimacy had been honed and reforged before the meeting she was both dreading and longing for finally came. The man had chosen to make her wait, but that could have been a tactical error on his part she hoped he was shortly going to regret. The connection between her and Will had become even stronger these last few days while Mr Greystone proved *he* did not run about at a woman's bidding. Helena felt sorry for any lady who tangled themselves up with such a genuinely cold fish. She might not have met him yet, but he must be that icy to do what she was very nearly sure he had done to a friend and fellow officer.

'It might not be the vicar,' she warned him hastily as Will went towards the front door and the wide hallway to bid their visitor welcome, even if he didn't want anyone coming here and risking bringing his enemy in after them. She felt as if old secrets and lies were about to come between them and wondered if even a love like theirs was strong enough to weather so many hard truths all at once.

'What have you done, Helena?' Will asked her bleakly as he listened to the voices outside and maybe he had already untangled his supposed friend's quieter one from Owain's shouts and stamping about to warn them a stranger was here.

She felt the dire threat to their happiness she had dreaded glowering at her and shook her head until her hair threatened to tumble down. Never mind, she was not going to fuss over her appearance and allow a monster to steal even one more moment from the future she had promised herself and Will. She still didn't quite believe that future was truly possible now the time had come to test it and fear was souring in her belly as she both dreaded and longed for this encounter to be over once and for all.

'Something that needed doing,' she argued, raising her chin to meet her husband's hot and angry dark eyes full on because what was the point of lying that this was not her doing when lies had done so much damage already?

'Nothing matters more than your safety and we had that well in hand between us until you dragged him here,' he barked at her so furiously she shivered in her ancient shoes. 'Why the devil must you always interfere?'

'Because somebody has to,' she said with her nose in the air even as she longed for him to simply trust her. He probably never would again after she had done this without even telling him about her doubts about his friend and the man's motives for helping him five years ago. Because he would not have listened, she reminded herself. He seemed blindly loyal to Mr Greystone and look what that loyalty had already cost him, so heavens send opening his eyes to the man's true character would not break Will just a little bit more and them along with it.

'You did not tell me he was coming,' he accused and apparently the temper blazing back at her from his stern dark eyes was one more fiery emotion they had unlocked together these last few days. She would have to learn to live with it flaring hot and reproachful at her as she refused to lower her own eyes and be ashamed of herself. She had gloried in all the other passions they'd aroused in one another while they discovered and greedily relearned one another. Even the fiery anger looking back at her seemed preferable to the iced-over version of him she had encountered in Edward's book room the day her whole world changed.

'I knew you would not agree to this meeting, although we needed it to happen before any of us can move on with our lives.'

'So you lied to me,' he challenged as if that was a worse betrayal than the wicked one she was trying to expose. He seemed to have forgotten all about their visitor as his bitter accusation bit into her certainty they were strong enough and close enough to weather any storm that hit them now.

'Never as thoroughly as you did to me or for anywhere near as long,' she said haughtily and knew this was her grand throw of the dice and she wasn't as unlike her late papa as she had always hoped. The late Lord Pensham's daughter seemed to have risked her all on a last throw of the dice as well and the risk of it felt sickening right now. She could not even think it might cost her everything she valued most in the world until her gamble was over and done with. Even then she would fight for her lover and their marriage because if the last few days had taught her anything it was where there was life there was still hope.

'Yes, I lied, but to keep you safe,' he said with such anguish in his voice she could not keep the distance between them any longer while they faced the man she had summoned here deliberately, even if Will wanted her to.

'And I would rather have stood openly at your side all this time than be kept safe in an ivory tower like a princess who needed guarding from hungry dragons, my love,' she told him as she sped across the room to take his resisting hand in hers. 'You did not give me any choice about that either and I missed you so badly while I was up there.'

For an awful moment she felt him withhold

closeness from her and she felt icy and sick at the shock of that cold wall between them after days of such glorious warmth and intimacy. Only her own steely pride stopped her shivering and letting him see and feel how much it hurt her to be aloof from him again, but then she felt his stiff hand relax in hers and he curled his long, strong fingers around hers as if he could not stop them clinging to hers. The shivers stopped as their warmth breached his stony barriers again and she let out her pent-up breath in a relieved sigh.

'Ah, Mr Greystone,' she greeted the new-comer confidently and coolly before Will could greet him as a friend.

'Lady Helena,' the man said after only the slightest of checks in his smooth step to say he was disconcerted by her cool stare and the fact Will was holding back from a more friendly greeting with his hand so firmly locked in his wife's he could not spare it for his old friend.

'You must have received my letter after all,' she informed rather than asked him.

She would not let Greystone subvert one more truth between her and Will. Now the man was here and so smoothly impassive, she knew she had been right about him all along. This man could lie with a straight face if there were a dozen bishops lining up to challenge him. She could see where Will had learned to hide his feelings behind the cold armour he wore when they met again, but this man's chilly gaze warned her not to expect any warmth or compassion hidden behind *his* icy façade.

'Indeed,' he said warily.

'You were very slow in replying, but at least you are here now,' she said and felt Will grow restless at the tone of this prickly encounter between his wife and an old friend. She shot Will a pleading look to say *trust me*. He clearly thought she was being rude, but nodded faintly and waited to find out why she was behaving as she was. Warmth flooded through her because he had faith in her doing what she felt was right even with this man he had trusted so much.

'I am at your service now I am here, my lady,' Greystone lied as he warily eyed their joined hands and gave her a slight bow, as if to acknowledge she had achieved a small victory before he arrived so tardily, even if he was quite certain he would win the battle.

'Excellent, then do come inside and shut the door behind you, sir,' she urged him coolly. 'I am quite sure you will not wish our conversation to be overheard.'

'Come now, my dear, surely we must offer him refreshments after such a long journey?' Will protested, but he still did not wrench his hand from hers to ring the bell himself and send for some, so maybe he had already realised deep down that this was too serious a matter for the social niceties.

'No,' Helena said implacably.

If she was right about this man, she would not give him any incentive to stay here a moment longer than he must and she did not want to break bread with him either. She let an uneasy silence stretch between them and willed Greystone to meet her eyes, but even when he did there was nothing in them to give a clue to his real feelings.

'Mr Greystone has had a very leisurely journey here,' she added, 'unlike ours as we scrambled along as best we could with you so worried about the devil on your tail, Will.

Therefore Mr Greystone cannot be as hungry or tired or thirsty as we were when we finally got here over a week ago now. We came over the mountains in such a pother we barely stopped for breath, let alone food or sleep, you see, Mr Greystone. My husband believed he was being pursued by his old, vengeful enemy and was quite determined to protect me from his nemesis now the war is finally over and you do not need him to pretend to be dead any longer so he has no cover from his enemies.'

Mr Greystone, pretending to be unassuming, came fully inside the sunny oak-panelled room at last and closed the ancient and heavy door on anyone who might decide to listen. He raised a seemingly amused eyebrow at Will as if to say how on earth did he tolerate his wife's virago-like ways and what the devil was wrong with him for doing so while she raged at such an old friend?

'You seem quite capable of protecting yourself, Lady Helena. You always were set and determined on getting your own way and to hell with the rest of us though, were you not? I must say, time and a very secret grief do not seem to have changed you in any of the essentials so maybe you are incurable.'

She sensed he knew he had made an error by striking out at her from the flicker of annoyance on his narrow patrician features before he controlled them ruthlessly again and blanked it out. His casual reference to her grief-haunted and horribly empty years without Will was meant to wound her and it had, but it also showed her he was far more worried than he was pretending to be by her threat to use both hers and Will's connections to stir up a hornet's nest for him if he did not come here within the week to meet her challenge.

'Have we met before?' she said and narrowed her eyes at him to search her memory for a younger version of the man, but she still came up with a blank.

'I am not surprised you do not recall it since you were so very busy with my dashing friend here at the time, Lady Helena,' he said so lightly she was sure her lack of recall had offended him.

Good, she was glad he hated being ignored then and now. If she was right, he had already offended her beyond any chance of human forgiveness and she was never saintly enough to even want to forgive him to start with. Ah, she had it—she had delved deep enough into the past and had to bite back a gasp as the man flitted over it like a grey fog.

He *was* there the first night she met Will, a blurred and unimportant background to the life-changing event that was Will's advent in her life. It was clear he had hated being ignored by them even that first night when everyone else faded next to Captain Harborough and his intense, intent dark brown eyes so hot on hers it felt as if they were the only two people in the world for a whole evening.

This man was the sceptical sniff meant to cast doubt on what he was beholding, the vague shadow that had only made Will seem all the more vivid and powerful by contrast as they gazed at one another as if there was nobody else in the room and the whole of the gossiping *ton* were blind to their locked gazes. How wrong they were, she recalled now and wondered if it would have made any difference to all their lives if she was a little less dazzled by Will and a lot more pleased to see his shadowy friend that fateful evening.

'I had clean forgotten you were with me on the night I first met my fate, Grey,' Will said as if he was still recalling a happy time with an old friend. But he held fast to her hand even so and that gave Helena enough courage to carry on.

'Grey! Of course, that's what you called him that night, Will. I recall another officer with you now that you have jogged my memory,' she said, calling up the image of a slight man dressed in a darker, less-familiar uniform than Will's scarlet and gold-frogged coat. Will's rakish smile and the very interested glitter in his dark eyes had blocked every other detail of that night from her mind until this very moment, especially since they had sneaked into the garden to kiss so blatantly her father caught them at it and threatened to call Will out if he dared dishonour his daughter ever again.

'You both forgot me easily enough that night, as well as the rest of the world,' Greystone said with a shrug he clearly hoped appeared indifferent. 'You two were so absorbed in one another that the clap of doom could have sounded and you would have simply shrugged and gone on staring at each other like Romeo and Juliet.'

'Luckily for us, you had no poison handy to turn it into a tragedy, then,' she said, and if the man thought it a joke he was mistaken. He did not think so, from the even more expressionless look he wore while he watched Will frown and look vaguely puzzled. She thought Greystone was trying to gauge how much of the past he could bluff away as if it had nothing to do with him under the air of injured innocence.

'You wanted her for yourself, didn't you?' Will asked him with such revulsion Helena held her breath and waited for her dear lover to turn back into the stony warrior she encountered in her brother's sitting room ten days ago.

'Of course I didn't, you damned fool.' Mr Greystone said and looked so genuinely revolted by the idea the world would ever be well lost to love that Helena believed him. 'I thought you two must have seen sense and backed away from one another just as Lord Pensham ordered you to,' Greystone told Will. 'I believed your act of pretend indifference whenever you two were together in public after that night. It was a damned good one and we both knew Lady Helena was way above your touch. I thought you both regretted that moment of lunacy and I can assure you I had no idea you were still so infatuated you rashly married in secret.'

The man must be clever to do what he had in the Peninsula and afterwards, but he was not very perceptive about the deepest of human passions, Helena decided as she looked back on the sly glances and furtive touches she and Will thought they were so secretly exchanging under cover of a terrible crush in a ballroom, or a fleeting meeting and averting of eyes, as if they had only encountered one another by accident and wished they didn't have to recall a night of mutual folly.

Anyone truly interested in his friend's well-being would have seen that they were lying through their teeth from the flush of colour in her cheeks and the gloating, anticipating sparkle in their eyes when they plotted by subtle ways and means how to meet in secret at nearly every ball and soirée of the heady, precious time of their furtive courtship.

'And to think I believed a truly effective spymaster must see behind the actions of others to gauge the emotions underneath them until I met you, Mr Greystone,' she said. She refused to let him belittle their love as a hasty infatuation followed by the even worse folly of marrying one another in secret.

'Well, *I* certainly did not gauge either of yours. I had no idea you were wed to anyone until you shouted about a wife in your sleep one day, Harborough,' the man said grimly and as if he held him very much to blame for having one.

'I did? Ye gods, I could have endangered you even more than I already had by marrying you, Helena,' Will said as if he was desperately ashamed of not being in full control of his dreams and needed to apologise for having any.

'Luckily you were in such a high fever nobody else would go near you because they thought you must be contagious,' Mr Greystone went on as if such a display of emotion was distasteful. 'You were stuck in a cave well away from your villainous friends when I tracked you down after you had missed our meeting.

You were shivering like a whipped dog and swearing like a trooper while you had nightmares about some man who had married your wife because she thought you were dead. Just as well it was mc who found you, since you were raving about what you would do to your rival in English and yelling insults at the wife I had no idea you even had until that very moment. You didn't name her even at your most feverish, so I still had no idea who she was.'

'Or you would never have done what you did, Mr Greystone?' Helena asked him sceptically.

'Certainly not,' the man said as if she was being ridiculous to even suggest it, but she thought it was yet another lie.

'You used the fake threat against Will's loved ones in order to make him agree not to argue with a false report of his death in battle you intended to make anyway. You turned my husband into a steely ghost of his former self, a scavenger after secrets, Mr Greystone. And you did it with a great big, guilty lie— your clever story that a wicked avenger had gone after Lady Aurelia Harborough with such tragic consequences. How convenient her death at the hands of an insanely jealous lover must have been for you and what an ideal starting point it was to your tall story. You put intolerable pressure on Will to make him do exactly what you wanted, Mr Greystone. He was your biggest asset in your bid to become indispensable to your commander-in-chief, was he not?'

'What? No, he couldn't have done all that and certainly not for the sake of advancement. You're wrong, love, Grey protected me and saved my life more than once. How can you say he used me for his own ends when it cost him so much to keep me hidden for so long?'

Will shook his head and ran his free hand through his close-cropped curls so they stood on end. How dearly she longed to reach up and smooth them down, to reassure him that the rock under his feet was firm as ever and not dissolving into sand as they spoke simply because his friend was false as Satan.

'Tell her, Grey; tell her you had already asked me to go deep under cover to use my command of the Spanish language more effectively than I ever could as an observing officer. I refused time after time, but in the end, I went *to him* to beg for some way out of the hell I was facing if that bastard killed you as well, Helena, not the other way about. I received those anonymous threats of vengeance after the traitor I unmasked by accident was shot. A couple of scrawled messages and a whispered threat outside my tent in the middle of nowhere to make me distrust everyone I encountered, but it was only when I got news of my mother's death that I finally had to take them seriously. If the writer did destroy everyone I loved so I knew how it felt to lose what I cared for most, I would be better dead than knowing you were dead because of what I had done. Grey could not have fabricated the whole rotten business; the very idea is absurd.'

'When did you contract that fever, Will?' Helena asked. His doubts were beginning to hurt despite their still locked-together hands.

Watching him go back over that time, the horror of dreading getting word that a wife nobody was supposed to know he even had was murdered like his mother made her feel as if she was experiencing it as well. She felt even more furious with the oddly insubstantial man who had come here so determined not to

yield her an inch in their struggle for Will
trust, but she was so full of love and pity
Will, harried into a terrible dilemma by th
unscrupulous rogue she just wanted the
gone from both their lives for ever.

'In the summer of the year 1813,' Will s
as if he was finally realising that was a lo
time ago as well. 'The Battles of the Pyren
were being fought all around us and I nee
to be fit and useful instead of languishin
a cave raving at you and an imaginary lov
he told her with a weary twist of humo
that made her want to cry, but of course
couldn't do that in front of such a cold cy
or Will when he was about to be devast
by the truth if only he could finally acce

'Two years ago, then,' she pointed out
stead. 'An unforgivable gap of time for yo
keep such a secret from a friend you had
in danger in the first place, don't you th
Mr Greystone?'

'There was nothing else I could do but
tend I did not know your secret, Harboro
Wellington needed all the information
could get when we were so close to pus

the French out of Spain that I could almost smell it.'

'What about afterwards, Mr Greystone? There seems such a lot of it yet to be accounted for.'

'I had to find out who he was wed to before I could put anything right.'

'And if only it was that simple,' Helena muttered sarcastically, but Will was too intent on his own dawning horror to take much notice.

'*You* were behind the so-called burglary at Deepdale only weeks ago, were you not?' he demanded and if Mr Greystone did not have the sense to shudder at Will's hurt fury Helena did it for him.

'Yes, I had to know who you were wed to if I was to stand any chance of helping you put things right with your wife, Will,' the man said as if he might still manage to bluff his way past far worse sins than a little bit of handy forgetfulness.

'You were there the first night we met; you must have had a strong suspicion I was the one Will married in secret. He had no chance to do so after he returned to his regiment and fell into your clutches, did he?' Helena pressed at an open door and saw Will accept what she said as true and glare at the man as if he had never truly seen him before.

'Why would I think of you, Lady Helena?' Greystone asked as if he thought he had every right to dismiss her and the wonder he had seen in both their eyes that heady night in Mayfair. 'You have not moved in polite society since your father died and you were very adept at concealing your feelings beforehand. For all I knew it could have been that lovely *hidalga* you sighed over in Madrid before Corunna, Will, or the pretty Portuguese piece you flirted with in Lisbon. Or you could have been dragooned into marrying any one of the silly girls who used to flock round you like chattering starlings whenever we were stationed anywhere in this country before we even got to the Peninsula.'

Helena always knew Will had had a wild reputation with the opposite sex before they met and so this was not the time to feel a roar of hot jealousy at that string of amorous adventures before they met.

'So, just to get this straight in my head, Mr Greystone, you admit that it was you who broke into Lord Flamington's strong room because you were looking for proof of who Will was actually married to?' she prompted, mainly to let him know his diversionary tactics had not worked.

'Yes, Will told me before we went into France this spring that his uncle knew he was alive and held his will. You wanted me to know in case anything happened to you if you remember, Will? I knew you would have named your wife in it to make sure she was provided for if you happened to be killed behind enemy lines for real this time.'

'Not exactly the actions of a gentleman,' Helena said flatly.

She could see Will was finally letting himself see what this man had done to them both for his own ends for so many years. His face was set and stony as the careless evil this man had done—and apparently with a clear conscience—hit him full on. Greystone had clung to his unpleasant, destructive scheme long after he knew how awful that threat to kill Will's loved ones really was. She could not look at the man to see what he thought of Will's dawning revulsion because he wasn't the one who mattered to her. This deep a betrayal would hurt Will to his very bones. He had already been hurt so badly by this soulless so-called friend she dreaded the full bitterness of Will's reaction to everything he had believed in for so long crumbling into dust around him.

'You made it all up, didn't you?' Will said with such a blank face Helena pressed herself against him to share her warmth. 'There was no thwarted lover or grieving father or a brother waiting to take twisted revenge on me for uncovering a traitor's sins. Only you, Grey, so ruthlessly determined to get your own way by any means you could find to use against me,' Will ended with such cold disgust even Helena shuddered.

'I needed someone inside the guerrilla bands to gain their trust as far as they ever trusted anyone. There was nobody better suited to the task than you, Will. You spoke the language like a native and even managed to get inside the Spanish factions that supported the French invasion and the supposed liberties Bonaparte offered them to find out if they were a threat to the Allies.

'You were a great asset to the Duke and I needed your continued help even after I found out you were wed. Your country needed your help, but you kept on refusing my offers and pleas to become a clandestine agent for my commander-in-chief and I was desperate. I did what I did so we could find out things we badly needed to know and once everyone believed you dead and buried after Bussaco nobody would look for a Spanish-speaking Englishman who was already supposedly in his grave.

'The cover was perfect. Nobody ever suspected you were my uncannily accurate source of information inside the guerrilla bands. Or at least they didn't until you came back to life again. Lucky for me you did not do that until a few weeks ago instead of when I needed information more than ever this spring.'

'After you inherited New Court from your great-uncle and no longer needed Wellington's approval to further your furtive career as well,' Will said bitterly. 'How very conveniently it has all turned out for you. You are a propertied gentleman so it hardly matters that no further advancement will be coming your way.'

Greystone shrugged indifferently as if there was no point in him even pretending he was ever in this for Will's sake now he had been seen through. Will was quite right, he had what he had always wanted so what did it matter if the truth of his betrayal of his supposed oldest friend was public knowledge or not? Helena wondered how much Spanish gold or French plunder he took during his furtive service, but it hardly mattered next to the melodrama he had set up to ruin both their lives for five long and very painful years.

'You turned me into a ghost, Greystone,' Will added, sounding so sadly stung by what had truly happened Helena almost wished it had not had to come out so painfully for him. 'You made me into a shadow, a nothing. I was a furtive, sneaking cur without a home or even a country for so long and all the time my wife believed I was dead it felt worse than torture. To think how grateful I was to you for finding a way to protect my loved ones from a devil and give me enough peace of mind to wake up every morning and not be terrified my wife had been brutally murdered in her bed last night exactly as my mother was.

'Fool that I was, I trusted you, Greystone. I believed every rotten self-serving lie you fed me like a slow-acting poison. I was grateful you saved my life not once, but twice. I could have died in that cave if you did not stay and force water down my throat and make sure a fire burned all night. I would have died inch by inch if a murdering bastard found out about Helena and killed her for the sweetest revenge on me a man could take. What was the point of living if she was dead and it was my fault? But there was never a threat, was there? I have never even stopped to think things through properly until this very moment and what a credulous fool that makes me.'

'Never mind, my love—why would a man like *you* think such casually evil things were even possible from a friend?' Helena stood on tiptoe to whisper in his ear and try to soothe his fury, even if it was directed at Greystone because she knew how much Will was hurting. 'We are both alive and safe,' she added. She felt as if something had shifted when he squeezed her hand and a whole new world seemed to open up in front of them with the darkness finally out of their lives.

'What you did to me was both conscience-less and wicked, Greystone, but I can never forgive you for what you did to my wife. I never want to set eyes on you again as long as I live, so kindly make sure that I do not. Goodbye.'

'But, Will...' the man blustered as if he had finally realised a future earl had just become his implacable enemy and maybe questions would be asked in high places about his conduct in the late wars as well.

Will marched to the door and Helena went with him because she wasn't letting go of his hand now and that meant going wherever he went. When they got there, he hastily opened the door and bellowed, 'Owain!' in a parade ground order.

'Yes, Mr Harborough,' his right-hand man said, sauntering into view as if he and the entire household had not been doing their best to listen through several frustrating inches of solid old oak door ever since it was shut on them. If Helena was not so disturbed by what had happened on the other side of it, she might have to admire the speed with which they must have whisked themselves out of the wide hallway.

'See Mr Greystone off my land and let it be widely known he is not welcome here ever again, if you please.'

'Gladly, sir,' the powerfully built Welshman said with a theatrical leer at the much slighter and not very powerful man who was trying to stare him down as if he was so inferior he hardly even existed. 'Come on then, my lad, jump to it,' he said with a hard look to let Greystone know there was a big *or else* behind his order.

'But...'

'Come on now, that's enough of your nonsense, quick march,' Owain ordered and Helena realised he must have been a soldier as well, once upon a time.

She watched Greystone marched away like a prisoner under guard and for some reason the whole horrible situation struck her as exquisitely funny. It must be shock and relief that she had been proved right and Will had believed her rather than an old friend. It still felt important for her to watch the carriage leave with Greystone staring out of the opposite window, as if he did not care to even think about his former friend any more and especially not his friend's wife.

Once he was gone, Owain was tasked with riding around the area spreading word the master of the house was not dead after all, but very much alive and back where he belonged. He looked as if he was glad to make sure Greystone never got as much as a greeting from the locals if he ever tried to come here again as well.

Chapter Seventeen

Helena went back into the house after her last glimpse of the anonymous-looking carriage as it rounded the last bend in the drive down to the valley floor and the road to somewhere else. She hoped it was the last time she ever set eyes on the man and at least now she and Will could live their lives without him being constantly haunted by his fears for her. She really wanted Castle Eyrie to be their home, but if Will wanted to live at Deepdale with his uncle she would make herself happy there instead. She would live in a cave if it had Will in it.

'You must have suspected he was a conscienceless fraud from the first time I told you why I had gone missing for so many years,' Will challenged her the moment they were back inside the drawing room with that solid oak door firmly shut behind them.

'Yes,' she admitted warily. So much for them being safe and even more united after outfacing his manipulative former friend together. There was such a cold sort of fury in his eyes now that he almost made her wish he was still intent on protecting her from imaginary assassins for a shocking moment.

'And you said nothing,' he added flatly.

'You would not have believed me,' she replied and knew that was the real reason she'd never told him about her doubts about his story and his friend. She did not want to risk him staring at her as if he didn't even want to know her, let alone be married to her, as he was doing now.

Only moments ago she had naively believed Greystone's days of coming between them were finally over. Now the old stony shield between her and Will was back and it made him look so grim and unlike his true self again she shivered and wondered bleakly where her impassioned lover of the past few glorious days had gone.

'How do you know? You didn't even try to

convince me the man I trusted so stupidly and for so long was beneath contempt.'

'And would you have taken my word against him after all you thought he had done for you?'

Will began to argue some hasty sort of yes, then stopped himself and marched to the bank of elaborately latticed windows to stare out of them at yet another golden afternoon as if he now demanded absolute honesty even from himself and he could not be that sure.

Who says it always rains in Wales? an oddly detached little voice asked at the back of her mind, while she tried not to stare longingly at the back of his grey-flecked head and maybe give herself away in a reflection in the finely polished glass.

'Probably not,' he admitted with his back to her.

'There we are, then—you trusted your friend more than you did your wife. It seems I was quite right to stay silent and wait for him to come here and condemn himself.'

He shifted as if his trust in such an unscrupulous man before his own wife made him acutely uncomfortable, but he didn't argue with her version of events. 'What is left between us if we cannot trust each other, Lady Helena?' he asked as if he thought she did not trust him enough when it seemed the other way round to her. 'You kept your doubts to yourself and let me go on believing in a threat that had only ever existed in my head and Greystone's chilly imagination if you were right.

'You have told me so many times how much you love me since we came here, and made hot, sweet love with me time after time while deep down you knew you were treating me like a child and I stupidly went along with it. I have been a deluded fool from start to finish, but you had me living a fairy tale while you were waiting for Greystone to strip me of my last few illusions.'

'You are not a fool, Will,' she corrected him more gently than he deserved. 'I could only see through his lies because I was on the outside of them all the time you were wrapped up in his furtive world, living with the belief that your mother was murdered to punish you and thinking I could be next.'

'Standing here now, that naive idiot who took Greystone's word for anything looks like the village idiot to me. What of my pride, though, Helena? What about the joint enterprise you promised yourself and me one fair morning in April all those years ago? How many of them were you willing to overlook to unravel me like this?'

'How can you say that after I mourned for you in secret for five long years *and* stayed silent about my absent husband for even longer?' she almost whispered because he was accusing her of not living up to their marriage vows and she refused to even admit to herself how deeply that hurt.

'Marriage is not just about four legs in a bed and cleaving only unto your husband, Helena. It is about mutual trust and confidence and comfort, about never holding back and keeping dark secrets from one another and never mind all those lusty outpourings of love without the rest of a true marriage to back them up.'

'What about the huge secret you kept from me for five years?'

'I thought it was the only thing that kept you truly safe, but it is clear now that it will always stand between us. You are always going to look at me and wonder if I told you the truth about the time I was wound up in Greystone's lies like a fly in a web. You obviously don't trust me and I simply can't live like that, Helena, not with you.'

'So let me get this straight in my head—first you would not have believed me ahead of your false friend and now you don't trust me to see past your sad charade to the real man underneath it and love you anyway?'

'How could you?' he said as if he thought it was impossible and that felt sadder than anything he had said so far.

'I don't know,' she said just as flatly. She had her pride as well and she refused to promise him anything he wanted just to make him see past his fury that she did not confide in him about her doubts the moment she felt them coming on.

'You cannot,' he said blankly as he turned to face her again with the same flat lack of expectation he had worn the first time they met again.

'I could if—'

'Don't bother with ifs, Helena. I am too savage to listen to any of them right now,' he burst out. At least it was passion, just not the sort she had got so used to seeing in his eyes these last few days. 'I have to get away from here, from you. I need to be alone again and think all this through without you there to distract me and drive me daft with needing you.'

'*Needing* me?' she asked, offended if that was all it was. 'Just willing to make up those four legs in a bed, Husband?'

'Only you can say if that is all it was and I can't take your word for it, can I?' he said and strode towards the door as if not being able to do that was a worse torture than his five years of lying that he was dead to protect her from a threat that it turned out had never even existed.

'Where are you going?' she demanded because he looked so wild and reckless now that she dreaded what he might do.

'Away. I need to climb mountains and shout at the void and convince myself I am fully and truly alive at last. I want to do all the things a man can when he knows his wife is safe from creeping assassins. I must learn to be Will Harborough again without anyone standing by my side telling me how to do it.'

'And what am I supposed to do while you stamp about doing all that?'

'Maybe you should do the same.'

'But not with you?'

'No, I can't think straight when I am with you and maybe you can't either.'

'Maybe not,' she said and it was her turn to stare blindly out of the window now. She refused to watch him leave the room or interfere when she heard him running upstairs to grab whatever he wanted to take with him. 'Take care, my love,' she whispered to the suddenly very heavy-feeling late summer air with autumn already on its heels.

Will already knew he was worse than the fool he felt when he finally realised what a gullible idiot he had been all these years. He had turned his fury at his stupidity and Greystone's betrayal on his wife. The dumb truth was he had been stupid with rage because he could not pound a smaller, lighter man with his fists until Greystone felt his sins the only way that might make him sorry about them.

Being raised a gentleman ought to have

made Will loathe his wife's empty years of not being a wife at all even more instead of raging at her for not confiding in him when she was right, he probably would have refused to believe her. It might have planted a seed to save him being a complete fool when Greystone's chilly soul was laid bare by his clever wife.

Will stared at the next rugged peak in his driven series of them and still turned his face away from the south and home. It was home because she was there—if he had not driven her away with his temper and pride and stupidity—and because it felt like one in a way vast and impressive Deepdale probably never would. Yet he still turned his face away from it and his wife and stormed on as if he was truly driven by demons.

He was more of a fool with every step he took away from her, but how could he simply turn around and go back now? He had hurt her even more than he'd managed to already with all those lies and a woman could only stand so much hurt before she gave up on her apology for a husband and asked for that legal separation after all.

His heart sank even as he smiled ruefully

at the idea of headstrong Lady Helena as a meekly suffering saint. There was nothing of the patient, put-upon and yet uncomplaining wife about her. He recalled how impatient and demanding she could be and was mighty relieved he was alone on the latest mountain path since a picture of her very impatient for his husbandly attentions in their latest marital bed was rendering him unfit for any sort of company but hers—if she was ever willing again after he had taken out his hurt and fury on her.

He should have bitten his tongue out first. It felt as if a small part of his self-serving tirade had been right, though. He must come to terms with the past before he could be the man he wanted to be with her in the future he realised he would now have to beg her to share with him.

At Greystone's bidding, Will had inflicted the grief and loneliness he saw in Helena's self-contained face and pared-down curves that first day at Hawley for no reason—no, that was wrong, the reason was Greystone's ambition. A vicious rage clenched his fists and made Will growl at the majestic view when he reached the peak of his latest mountain instead of being awed and humbled by the rugged majesty of this part of his great-grandmother's country. Until he could put the dark secret life he had been fooled into living firmly in the past where it belonged, he would not be fit for the better life he must beg Helena to let him live with her now.

Whether she was still at Castle Eyrie or back at Hawley, or even with Lady Herridge in Derbyshire, he needed to find her and throw himself at her feet until she was tired of walking over him. He had to believe she would forgive him one day, that she was a better person than he would ever be. If he grovelled hard enough and for long enough, maybe she would let him back into her life because it would never have true meaning if he had to live without her for the rest of it because of his endless stupidity.

It had now been nearly as many days since Will had left her so lonely here as they had spent together after he returned to her from the dead. The hours and days had spun past at such a dizzying speed when he was here, but they seemed to drag like heavy weights now he was gone. Missing him so much during all those heavy-footed days and hours and minutes was witless of her and she had no idea why she was even still here. After reaching out to her closest friend, she had had a reply from Kate saying to visit her at Herridge Hall and at least make the silly man come all the way there to find her.

There were also several furious missives from the Dowager Countess ordering her errant daughter to come home and explain her sins to her mother in person since Edward had been forced to reveal them when whispers of Lady Helena's secret marriage began to circulate among the *ton*. Greystone had obviously been busy, but if he thought it was a fit revenge on her for smoking him out, he was wide of the mark. Helena could only be proud of her husband and the extraordinary risks he had undertaken to keep his secret wife safe.

And she was proud of him, even if she still didn't quite know why she had stayed here. Probably because she could not bear to leave this lovely place that had felt so much like their home. She raised a slightly grubby hand to rub her breastbone as if that might take the soreness from her aching heart and shook her head impatiently because she knew all too well that it would not work by now.

She had spent too many years missing the dratted man so badly that sleep was elusive or tortured with nightmares of his ugly death on a faraway battlefield to believe anything could take that ache away but him. At least she knew from bitter experience how to blot him out with hard work and this time she knew he was not dead. Just losing himself somewhere, raging alone at the Fates and false friends and feeling stupidly guilty about someone else's sins.

When he could have stayed here and done it all with me, she told herself miserably, and wondered how that would have worked out.

Probably not that well, she decided, what with her and the household tiptoeing around him as he worked through his confusion and outrage. It seemed more than likely he would have slammed off in a fine temper to purge it on his own in the end anyway. But at least he might not have gone with such harsh words between them. Her heart began to ache all over again at the very thought of him saying them as if he meant every one.

She sighed because she knew deep down he had been right to do this alone. He really did need to learn how to be his true self again, to be true to the Will she knew he always was under the hard, cold shell deception after deception had forced him to wear. She told herself his furtive life had probably done some good and if he had only saved one British soldier, or Spanish guerrilla, or a family from the horrors even strong men could only whisper about behind their hands and shake their heads at the brutality of all out war, maybe it was worth it.

She wanted to tell him so, to soothe his guilt and rage and make him see himself as he really was, but she would not be used as his whipping boy. He would have to grovel until he convinced her he would never do it again before she offered him as much as a finger to kiss and never mind the rest of her.

'Mistress Catrin needs to know where you want the carpenters to start, my lady,' one of the new maids interrupted Helena's reverie and reminded her she was supposed to be sorting ancient lumber instead of missing her husband.

'They are here at last, that's good,' she replied, glad of a better distraction from the dratted man. She set them to work mending the elaborate linen-fold panelling in the master bedroom. Since she could not sleep in there on her own, they might as well start there while it was not being used.

The last of the daylight was fading from the western sky in a haze of glorious reds and apricots and September was already upon them. As she gazed out at the fading day, Helena recalled Will standing in this same place a fortnight ago and tried to distract herself from missing him more than ever. What if he slipped down some savage gap on a wild and uninhabited mountaintop? Even a mountain goat might stumble and lose its way in the remoter reaches of the untamed lands further north. He could be lying there hurt for days, injured or trapped, and nobody would know. She should have sent Owain after him or gone herself, or got a whole expedition together to find one stray and very angry missing gentleman.

Panic began to overcome the calm common sense she had tried to impose on herself from the moment he rasped out his harsh words all those days ago and stamped off in a rage. She should have made him take someone with him, someone who knew the remote and sometimes dangerous North Wales peaks much better than he did. Or he could have taken the sturdy cob he rode into this lovely valley on by her side what seemed like months ago now.

She was about to dash upstairs to search for her disreputable garb from their last adventure and hope Catrin had not given it away or used it for rags when she heard Will's distinctive steps striding across the hall leading from the back of the house as if he had never been away. She knew it was him as surely as if he had shouted her name.

Despite a singing sense of relief because he sounded quite unharmed, her heart raced with apprehension. What if he had let the wrong Greystone had done them fester while he was out in the hills and mountains brooding? What if he was hard and cold and unreachable again like that first day at Hawley when he looked like a stone statue of himself instead of her living, breathing husband?

'Helena? Helena, where the devil are you?' she heard him shout and panic slipped away with a relieved sigh. He sounded cross and weary and a bit anxious, but so much his true self she caught herself smiling at thin air before she straightened her face and marched out to glare at him like an angry fishwife.

'Where the devil do you think I am, you great buffoon?' she shouted back at him. 'Waiting for you like stupid Patience on her stupid monument, of course, that's where I am and what I have had to do since you left here like an angry bear more days ago than I care to count,' she lied even as her eyes searched the deepening shadows for a hint of some hurt he might have suffered in his driven quest to think his angry manly thoughts in angry manly solitude.

'There's no need to shout,' he said mildly, but he was so wrong.

'There is every need,' she snapped back and waved sad, self-denying and stupidly patient Lady Helena goodbye without regret. 'I thought you were injured or stuck somewhere impossible to find out there in the wilds on your own, you great fool. I was about to find my breeches and that horrible coat you made me wear on the way here and come after you on Pippin since you have been gone so long I feared something awful must have happened to you, you stupid oaf.'

'If I had known you might do that, I might have stayed out there a little bit longer,' he told her with a leer in his deep voice to say he liked the idea of seeing her in breeches again and how dare he?

He caught her flailing fist unerringly when she almost let her temper fully off the leash. 'You don't really want to hurt me, do you?' he murmured as their curious staff stayed discreetly out of the way, but she could practically feel them listening from the kitchen doorway. 'Not when your beloved is truly home from the wars and you love me so dearly you waited six and a half long years and another fortnight for the stupid oaf to come home to beg your forgiveness on his knees,' he said and folded her into a great bear hug whether she wanted one or not.

She stopped struggling and let him hold her until she felt truly warm again for the first time in two long weeks, because there was offended dignity and cutting off your nose to spite your face. Nevertheless, the fury and heartache and misery of the last few days soon reminded her he didn't deserve this much welcome from his yet-again deserted wife.

'Maybe I was too busy to notice you had gone and I won't let you march back in here like this, expecting to be welcomed as if you have never been away. Not after what you said and did to me before you left,' she told him as she managed to wrench herself away from his warmth and strength with a supreme effort.

'Have you stopped loving me?'

'Never you mind and don't even think about doing that again in the state you have got yourself in while you were gone,' she said as he grabbed at her again with a glint in his eye she could see even in the deepening twilight. 'Stay away from me, you ill-tempered beast,' she snapped and managed to dodge his next lunge even as her heart sang because he was back and he felt like her Will again.

If he had come back to her without the hard protective shell and grim shadows, maybe she could forgive his hot and hurtful words before he left her, yet again. If they found an echo of the warmth and laughter and love of that blissful, stolen week together all those years ago, maybe it was worth every second of this nerve-stretching fortnight. Maybe, but he had better not push his luck one iota more.

'Forgive me, my lady?' he said in a lightning change of mood. Then he knelt at her feet in the wide hall and grabbed her hand before she could whip it behind her back. He kissed it so passionately a shiver of awareness shook her whole body, but she refused to let it take her over. She needed words as well as actions to convince her he had finally walked his hurts and furies out of himself and did not intend to launch any more of them at her.

'I am not fit for you to wipe your feet on, Lady Helena. I railed at you like an idiot. That unforgivable lie hurt so much because I knew it was my fault. I was such a credulous fool and you saw straight through it,' he said very seriously.

She recalled her angry, hurting resolution to make him grovel and realised the future mattered more than hasty words spoken from hurt and grief for what they had lost for no real reason as much as temper. 'Not so,' she argued, Greystone's frigid sins looming between them for a moment, but she refused to let him spoil one more second of their lives together.

She ruffled Will's now not as brutally short dark curls because she couldn't help herself. She loved the familiar feel of them even as wildly windswept as they currently felt. She smiled a rather wobbly smile she doubted he could see through the ever-deepening gloom.

'I really do love you, Helena, with all of my oafish heart. I always have and I always will.'

'I know, now get up, you idiot, before you ruin your knees or your breeches,' she told him and tugged his hand to persuade him she preferred him upright and she did believe he truly meant it this time.

'I am nothing without you, Helena,' he said, still being serious as he stood up to loom over her again in the semi-darkness.

'No, you are someone, but we two are always better together than apart,' she said seriously as well.

'There are so many things I have to be sorry for, though, love. If we are to have the new start we promised ourselves, I must confess it all. I spent the months before Bussaco, while I was still officially alive, missing you and why on earth was I still too stubborn to write and beg you to join me and just trust we would both survive because I could not endure living without you much longer?'

'I don't know—why didn't you when it would have saved us both so much sorrow and misery? But you can do penance for that when we're not quite so busy working through why you railed at me like that before you stormed out,' she said, standing on tiptoe to feel instead of imagine his face in the darkness. 'You need a shave,' she told him as she felt the abrasion of the beard he had grown while he was away under her exploring hand.

'I do and what a fool you did saddle yourself with on that fine April morning all those years ago, my lady,' he said half seriously.

'True, you are also scruffy, windswept and in need of a bath and a lot of civilising.'

'Maybe if our staff had time to spare from eavesdropping on us they would have the time to help me do something about it.'

'An excellent idea and maybe some candles to let us see what a wild man you made yourself into while you were away would be a good idea as well.'

A few furtive whispers were followed by the sounds of several people being noisily busy and Will managed a gruff laugh for their antics. 'Do you think they have really gone?' he said.

'Yes, but they will soon come bustling back pretending to have been elsewhere all this time. My mother would be furious at me for allowing such goings on under my husband's roof if she knew what a terrible keeper of your castle I am,' she replied and dared to believe in the ease they were sharing under that very roof, the life it felt as if they were really going to live with one another here after all.

'*Our* castle and I like them far better than the "yes, sir, no, sir" sort of servants we are supposed to employ and hope you do too.'

'Of course I do. So much better for us to feel a part of something here instead of holding ourselves haughtily aloof. Can Lord Flamington's heir be happy here with such a lack of state and stateliness?'

'He can be happy anywhere you are. I managed to work that out while I was away, even if I did have to clump about the hills ranting at the Fates and false friends and my own gullibility until I was sane again. I missed you so much it felt like purgatory.'

'Good, because I did that, too, and I didn't deserve to be lonely and miserable.'

'We have a lot to make up for and perhaps we should start now,' he said and gave a great unfettered laugh when her rumbling stomach argued it needed filling first. 'Oh, the mundane reality of being man and wife, out in the open at long last,' he muttered in her ear.

'I love it, though you still need a bath and a shave and I still want my dinner,' she murmured as candles flared in the darkness when the maids bustled into the hall as if they had no idea the master and mistress of the house had been standing here in the twilight for far too long.

* * *

The atmosphere of the whole house felt lighter and warmer somehow, although nothing much had changed here since they came here when it was half asleep and without a proper owner. Yet for Will it must feel as if everything about his life had changed. He was free of the fear that had stalked him for so long and some of the weight of what he had seen and done had fallen from his shoulders. It made him seem taller and, yes, younger, as the mellow light of more candles than usual lit the highly polished table and reflected the silverware and flowers and there was an air of excitement about the place as well, as if Catrin and Cook had decided life had truly come back into this waiting old house at long last and it needed a celebration.

'Ah, this is the life for me,' newly bathed and shaved and almost civilised Will said as he escorted Helena to the place set next to his because they refused to shout down a whole refectory table's worth of space at one another.

'Our life,' she agreed as she sat down to eat her dinner next to her husband in their house

in this lovely, tucked-away valley in a nice remote part of Britain.

The *haut ton* were hardly likely to find them
here and intrude on Lady Helena Harborough
and her not very secret husband being dread-
fully unfashionable and so deeply in love they
didn't care what anyone thought about their
past, present or future because their life here
was just how they liked it.

Epilogue

'**D**'you think we are done this time, Helena?' Will asked his wife as he tucked the tiny sleeping infant into the crook of his arm and tried to pretend he wasn't every bit as besotted with their latest child as he was with all the others.

'Unless you are planning for us to sleep apart for the next decade or so I very much doubt it,' Helena said with a rather weary smile because, although she had had a good deal of practice at this now, giving birth was still a painful and exhausting business, despite the wonderful results.

'That is five boys now, though. They should be enough to keep even Uncle Peter happy about the Harborough succession he was so concerned about when he only had me left to hand anything on to.'

'I do love your uncle and you know how much I have come to value his good opinion, but not a single one of our boys was ever for him and his august title, Will. They were all born for their own sake.'

'I agree, although I am to tell you that young Peter is thoroughly disgusted with you for producing yet another brother. He told me to say he insists on a sister next time. For some strange reason he doesn't seem to relish being big brother to yet another addition to our unruly band of boys.'

'If he thinks girls are all sweetness and light, he may be in for a shock if he does get a sister next time,' Helena said with a wry smile at the thought of their sons being kept in order by a bossy little sister, as her own brother always swore he had been by her when they were children. 'I would like a daughter or two as well though, Will,' she said with a dreamy, loving smile for her latest offspring, nestled in his father's arms as if he already knew it was one of the safest places in the world for him to be.

'I shall have to see what I can do,' he said with such a fine imitation of a self-satisfied male who thought this was all his doing that she managed to find enough energy to swat his nearest arm with a weary fist.

'As if I have no say in the matter,' she told him sleepily and he grinned at the reminder of her very willing participation in begetting all five of their children so far.

She sighed with a blissful sort of contentment at how her life had turned out after all, then she fell asleep knowing Will had their latest son safe and he was as much of a wonder as all the rest of them. When you were the mother of five enterprising boys and wife to a charming, adventurous and very beloved man you needed all the rest you could get before it was time to rise from your bed and get the whole pack of them back into some sort of order again.

* * * * *

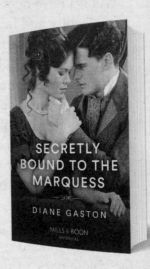

COMING SOON!

We really hope you enjoyed reading this book.
If you're looking for more romance, be sure to
head to the shops when new books are
available on

Thursday 27th
October

To see which titles are coming soon, please visit
millsandboon.co.uk/nextmonth

MILLS & BOON

MILLS & BOON®

Coming next month

THE LADY'S YULETIDE WISH
Marguerite Kaye

Then Eugene saw her. Petite, with a wild tumble of curly black hair pinned up in a top knot, clad in a dark dress with a white apron tied over the voluminous skirt. He told himself that it was merely the resemblance to a nurse's uniform that made him think it could be *her*, but his instant reaction was too visceral for him to be mistaken. He would never forget that one, fleeting memorable night.

He remembered the silky, springy texture of her hair when it tumbled loose over her shoulders. He remembered the olive tone of her skin, the voluptuous curves of her body, the full breasts, the flare of her hips. He remembered the roughness of her calloused hands on his skin. The tangle of their limbs, slick with sweat. The scent of their lovemaking mingling with the all-pervading smell of battlefield mud. The soft, muffled cry she made when she climaxed.

He remembered the flickering oil lamp in the makeshift wooden hut. The coarse sheets and inadequate blanket on the small bed. The open trunk, half packed with her belongings. He could vividly recall his last glimpse of her sitting up in the bed, the sheet clutched around her, as he picked up his clothing from the floor in the grey light of dawn. And that last, lingering kiss goodbye.

All this flashed through his mind in those seconds as he stood rooted to the spot, both entranced and shocked.

He had never thought to see her again, though their passionate night still haunted his dreams, nine months later. What the hell was she doing here? He had barely formulated the question when she turned. Heart-shaped face. Huge brown eyes under fierce brows. Full mouth which formed into an 'oh' of shock when she saw him. She stood perfectly still, absurdly rooted to the spot just as he was, the colour draining from her cheeks, before returning, colouring them bright red, as she hurried towards him, pushing him out of the door and back into the entranceway.

'Hello, Isabella,' he said, as if there was any doubt.

Continue reading
THE LADY'S YULETIDE WISH
Marguerite Kaye

Available next month
www.millsandboon.co.uk

MILLS & BOON

THE HEART OF ROMANCE

A ROMANCE FOR EVERY READER

MODERN

Prepare to be swept off your feet by sophisticated, sexy and seductive heroes, in some of the world's most glamourous and romantic locations, where power and passion collide.

HISTORICAL

Escape with historical heroes from time gone by. Whether your passion is for wicked Regency Rakes, muscled Vikings or rugged Highlanders, awaits the romance of the past.

MEDICAL

Set your pulse racing with dedicated, delectable doctors in the high-pressure world of medicine, where emotions run high and passion, comfort love are the best medicine.

True Love

Celebrate true love with tender stories of heartfelt romance, from the rush of falling in love to the joy a new baby can bring, and a focus on emotional heart of a relationship.

Desire

Indulge in secrets and scandal, intense drama and plenty of sizzling he action with powerful and passionate heroes who have it all: wealth, sta good looks…everything but the right woman.

HEROES

Experience all the excitement of a gripping thriller, with an intense ro mance at its heart. Resourceful, true-to-life women and strong, fearles face danger and desire - a killer combination!

To see which titles are coming soon, please visit

millsandboon.co.uk/nextmonth